Monsieur Pamplemousse Hits the Headlines

Monsieur Pamplemousse Hits the Headlines

MICHAEL BOND

This edition first published in Great Britain in 2006 by
Allison & Busby Limited
13 Charlotte Mews
London W1T 4EJ
www.allisonandbusby.com

Copyright © 2003 by MICHAEL BOND

The moral right of the author has been asserted.

A Catalogue record for this book is available from
the British Library.

10 9 8 7 6 5 4 3 2 1

ISBN 0 7490 8161 9
978-0-7490-8161-4

Printed and bound in Great Britain by
Bookmarque Ltd, Croydon, Surrey

Michael Bond was born in Newbury, Berkshire in 1926 and started writing whilst serving in the army during the Second World War. In 1958 the first book featuring his most famous creation, Paddington Bear, was published and many stories of his adventures followed.

In 1983 he turned his hand to adult fiction and the detective turned *gastronome par excellence* Monsieur Pamplemousse was born. This is the fourteenth book to feature Monsieur Pamplemousse and his faithful bloodhound Pommes Frites.

Michael Bond was awarded the OBE in 1997. He is married, with two grown up children, and lives in London.

Also by Michael Bond

Chapter One

History wasn't Monsieur Pamplemousse's strong suit, but when Pommes Frites sank his teeth into Claudette Chavignol's *derrière* which, as ill luck would have it happened to be *sans culottes* at the time, he couldn't help being reminded of the occasion in 1796 when Napoleon Bonaparte suffered a similar fate. It was the future Emperor of France's wedding night, and as he climbed into the marital bed, Josephine's pet dog Fortuné, thinking his mistress was about to suffer a fate worse than death, leapt to her defence.

It was probably the first, but not necessarily the last time Napoleon uttered the immortal phrase, "Not tonight, Josephine!"

There the comparison ended. The two *derrières* bore little resemblance to each other. Had he been asked to voice an opinion on the subject, Monsieur Pamplemousse would have said that fortune had smiled on Pommes Frites, whereas Fortuné had drawn the short straw.

He had no means of knowing if his faithful hound's spirited attack on Madame Chavignol had any after effects, although he doubted if many men had suffered as a consequence, but in Napoleon's case the experience certainly put him off dogs for the rest of his life.

In some respects the Emperor ought to have considered himself lucky. Pommes Frites weighed in at some 50 or so kilos. Had he landed on top of him, Josephine might have been impressed, but the whole course of history could have been changed.

These things were largely a matter of chance. Or were

they? Sometimes, past, present and future seemed to be inextricably intertwined.

In retrospect, Monsieur Pamplemousse often wondered if the circumstances leading up to his involvement in the gruesome affair of Monsieur Claude Chavignol's death in front of several million viewers had been preordained.

However, such thoughts were far from his mind that Sunday morning when he was heading for the Porte de Bercy and decided to take a short cut rather than stick to the main road. It was something he had done many times before over the years.

Indeed, on sunny weekends in late autumn, when all Paris seemed to be heading towards the Bois de Vincennes for one last day out, it was often his preferred route.

That said, it was a classic example of how, simply by obeying an impulse and turning a corner, one's whole life can be turned upside down. In retrospect, he sometimes tried to picture what might have happened had he carried straight on along the Rue Claude Decaen. Would the murderer have got away with it? He would never know for sure.

It was the first time he had ever met with any trouble turning off where he did. As it was, no sooner had he accelerated away from the junction in order to gain as much ground as possible, than he encountered a row of red warning arrows in the middle of the road. At the same time a *gendarme* emerged from behind a portable cabin and signalled him to pull in to the side.

It all happened so quickly several seconds passed before he applied the brakes.

Pommes Frites was taken by surprise too. Until that moment he had been happily enjoying the passing scene from the passenger seat. He looked most put out as he ended up with his chin on the dashboard.

Aware that he had come to rest several metres beyond the spot indicated by the *gendarme*, Monsieur Pamplemousse fully expected his emergency stop to be the subject of a verbal comment or two. Perhaps even a check to see when he'd last had his brake pads renewed.

Instead, the officer saluted politely as Monsieur Pamplemousse opened the window. There was no sign of recognition. He was probably too young to remember the face that had once graced the pages of a thousand *journaux*. Snapping to attention and saluting was fast becoming the exception rather than the rule.

'*Monsieur...*' clearly a man of few words, the *gendarme* directed his baton towards another figure emerging from the hut. Dressed in civilian clothes, he was hastily brushing some *croissant* crumbs from his trousers with one hand, while clasping a clip-board in the other. 'A few questions.'

'It will only take a moment or two.' The newcomer produced a ballpoint pen from his top pocket and clicked it open in business-like fashion. 'Now, you are travelling to where?'

'Melun,' said Monsieur Pamplemousse. 'Near Fontainbleau.'

'Business or pleasure?'

'Neither.'

The man raised an eyebrow. 'I have only two boxes, *Monsieur*. It is necessary to place a tick in one or the other.'

'I am visiting my sister-in-law.'

'Aaah!' The point was taken. His pen hovered momentarily over the clipboard. Even the most carefully thought-out forms had their grey areas.

'*Monsieur* is making a regular journey?' he asked hopefully.

'I make it as seldom as possible,' said Monsieur

11

Pamplemousse. 'Tell your superiors that if they are thinking of building an underpass based on your survey, it would be a poor investment of the tax-payers money to do so on my behalf.'

'There have been complaints from the local residents about the amount of through traffic.'

Monsieur Pamplemousse climbed out of his car and looked around. It struck him as being a particularly neglected part of the 12th *arrondissement*, but he resisted the temptation to say 'What residents?' The sooner the questions were answered, the sooner he would be on his way.

'I hardly think my contribution is of any moment,' he said. 'I travel this way perhaps two or three times a year at the most. I visit Melun to fetch my wife after she has been staying with her sister.'

'That is not how a statistician would view the matter, *Monsieur*,' said the man stiffly. 'Everything has to be taken into account. Only when all the relevant information has been collected and fed into the computer will the final result be known. But they are not infallible. A few years ago one threw up the suggestion that the only way to resolve the traffic problem on the Champs Èlysées would be to turn the Place de la Concorde into a pedestrian precinct. Imagine the uproar that would have caused.

'*Alors!* You would be surprised. Only yesterday we had a man who uses this road four times a day, five days a week, and has done so for the past fourteen years. It is his preferred route. Now, he would dearly love an underpass between here and the other side of the *périphérique*. It would probably halve his journey time.

'On the other hand, a few minutes ago a man passed through who was on his way to Iceland. It will be the trip of a lifetime. He won the holiday after entering a competition on the back of a packet of breakfast cereal. It is probably the only time he will ever pass this way. Looking on the dark side, should his luck change and he happens to meet with an accident while he is over there – slipping on some black ice, perhaps, or turning the thermostat up too high when he retires for the night in his igloo – we may never see him again.

'Then again, early this morning there was a lady who was on her way home from the 18th *arrondissement*. She works nights in the Pigalle area. She said she was dying to get back to her own bed in Ivry-sur-Seine and if I didn't keep her talking too long I was welcome to enjoy a quickie behind my hut...' He felt in his pocket. 'She left me these to distribute. I tell you, Monsieur, in this job you meet all sorts.'

Monsieur Pamplemousse hastily refused the proffered card. *'Merci beaucoup!* In any case, I am from the 18th myself.'

He felt a jolt as the *gendarme* kicked one of the back tyres. It was the time-honoured test. Fortunately he could detect no sound of escaping air. To have to change a wheel at this stage of the journey would be the last straw.

'And did you find a suitable box to tick?' he asked.

Ignoring the remark, the man glanced across at Pommes Frites and made an entry. 'Passengers...*un.*'

There was another jolt as the *gendarme* applied his foot to the nearside front tyre. He looked disappointed when nothing happened. 'You don't come across many 2CV's these days,' he said. 'In fact, I haven't seen one in years.'

Monsieur Pamplemousse couldn't help thinking there wouldn't be any left at all if the *gendarme* had his way. He was glad he had invested in Michelin radials. They could withstand anything that was thrown at them.

'Does the dog always travel with you?' asked the interviewer.

'Invariably,' said Monsieur Pamplemousse firmly. 'He performs a valuable service, especially on days like today. For *déjeuner* we will be having *tripes à la mode de Caen* and I shall need his help. My sister-in-law Agathe first served it to me many years ago when I was courting my wife. In order to gain favour I said it was the best I had ever eaten. She has been serving it to me ever since.'

The man looked up at him sympathetically. 'It is not good?'

'It is arguably the worst I have ever encountered,' said Monsieur Pamplemousse fervently. 'Agathe is a lovely person. She has a heart of gold. But she has two faults. She "enjoys" bad health and, unlike my wife, she is a terrible cook.'

'The two often go together,' said the *gendarme*, joining in the conversation. 'To be successful, *tripes à la mode de Caen* need a great deal of lengthy preparation. Ideally, the tripe should come from ruminants that have been fed in *guimaux* meadows, that is to say meadows bearing two crops of grass a year. The belly, the first and second stomach, along with a calf's foot, which of course should be split, the bone removed, then blanched, all need to be thoroughly washed in cold water. This is especially the case with the second stomach, which is honeycombed and can be a source of trouble. Then a flameproof casserole dish – preferably the flat type peculiar to Normandy – should be lined with sliced apple and onion. Reinette apples are supposed to be the best. The most important ingredients after that are carrots, onions, leeks, a *bouquet garni*, and of course cider, preferably dry from the Vallée d'Auge, with a few tablespoons of Calvados mixed in.'

Monsieur Pamplemousse revised his earlier assessment of the *gendarme*. He was clearly a man to be reckoned with.

'There are those,' broke in the man from the census

office, 'who say it is not necessary to put apple in the casserole. They say the best solution is to round off the meal with an apple tart afterwards.'

'I have an aunt who lives in Caen,' said the *gendarme* stiffly. 'I think she knows what she is talking about. She maintains the real secret is in the slow cooking.'

'It should be given at least twelve hours,' agreed the interviewer. 'Not a minute less. I, too, have relatives in Normandy,' he added, not to be outdone.

'I doubt if my sister-in-law gives hers more than two hours,' said Monsieur Pamplemousse. 'She turns the heat up high.'

'*Sacré bleu!*'

The *gendarme* crossed himself. 'If you ask me, short cuts are a symptom of a nation in decline,' he said gloomily. 'Everyone is in a hurry these days.'

As if to underline his words there came the sound of a horn. Glancing over his shoulder he glared at a Peugeot, the first in a growing line of vehicles, and signalled the driver to wait.

Monsieur Pamplemousse was tempted to point out that if the officer had been out directing traffic on the main road people wouldn't need to take a short cut, but he restrained himself.

'That is why we are conducting this survey,' said the interviewer, coming to his rescue. 'If a new bypass is built this road will no longer be a short cut.'

'I haven't looked in a *supermarché*,' he continued, 'but it wouldn't surprise me to find that many of them stock deep-frozen *tripes à la mode de Caen* these days.'

The *gendarme* shook his head sadly. 'Nothing is sacred. Full of additives no doubt. Along with instructions to give it three minutes in a microwave!

It is criminal.There are some things in life that can't be

15

hurried.'

'My wife's sister Agathe's *tripes à la mode de Caen* is not only a criminal offence,' said Monsieur Pamplemousse, 'it is also very grey.'

'Ah,' said the *gendarme*. 'Now that is possibly because she has not sealed the lid of the *tripière* properly. It needs to be done very thoroughly with pastry dough in order to preserve the whiteness of the intestines.'

'With respect, *Monsieur*, that need not necessarily be the cause.' The driver of the Peugeot joined in the conversation. 'Forgive me, but I couldn't help overhearing. The use of too much cider in the liquid is often a cause of blackening.

'The making of *tripes à la mode de Caen* is a construction job. The tripe itself needs to be cut into 5cm squares. The arrangement of the various layers is important. It is a case of building up from a generous bottom layer of onion to form the base, and then come the diced carrots followed by the leeks. After the meat has been arranged it should be covered with a layer of beef kidney lard before the cider is added.'

'I doubt if my sister-in-law adds any cider,' said Monsieur Pamplemousse gloomily. 'She may show it the label on an old bottle, but that's as far as she would ever go. Again, unlike my wife, she is teetotal.'

It was a conversation stopper.

'No Calvados?' asked the newcomer.

'*Pas de cidre*?' exclaimed the interviewer.

'Not even any *jus de parapluie*?' The *gendarme* used the slang term for cheap wine.

Monsieur Pamplemousse shook his head at all three possibilities.

'It is no wonder you don't go to see her very often,' said the interviewer. He clicked his pen shut. 'She would be better off buying it ready cooked from a delicatessen.'

There was a moment's silence as the others turned to look at each other in despair.

Catching Pommes Frites' eye, Monsieur Pamplemousse wondered if he should seize the moment to make a dash for it. He didn't feel it incumbent upon himself to apologise for his sister-in-law's shortcomings. He glanced pointedly at his watch. He could hear the steady hum of traffic in the distance and he was anxious to be on his way. At the rate they were going he must have lost several hundred places. It was worse than being sent back to *DÉPART* in a game of Monopoly.

But he had left it too late. The gesture was like water off a duck's back. The others were off again.

'These things,' said the Peugeot man, 'traditional recipes... must not be allowed to die out. Regional cuisine is what makes our country the way it is.'

'Such specialities are one of the joys of travelling in France,' agreed the *gendarme*. 'It is one of our great strengths. Part of our national heritage.'

'It is also the backbone of the tourist trade,' broke in the man from the census.

'I'm not so sure.' The Peugeot driver looked sceptical. 'The concept of regional specialities is foreign to Americans. Apart from that, they don't understand the joy of driving. To them a car is merely a means of getting from point A to point B as quickly as possible.'

'Not just Americans,' said another man who had just arrived on the scene.

'Take peas. There are many in France today who have never known the joy of running their thumb down a half open pod and watching the contents fall out.'

'There is a particular sound as they land in the vessel,' agreed a fifth. 'It is like that of rain falling on a tin roof.'

'I prefer broad beans,' said the Peugeot man. 'I love the furry feel on the inside of the pod – the little pockets for each bean.'

'My vote would go to the moment when you unearth the first of the new season's potatoes,' said the interviewer. 'There is nothing like it. It is how I always imagine prospectors must feel when they are panning for gold.'

'Most of all,' said Monsieur Pamplemousse, 'there is the joy of eating them. With freshly picked peas and beans there is the slight crunchiness of the outside, followed by the explosion of tastes from within.'

'There are those,' said the *gendarme*, 'who will never experience such things. I dare say they think they grow on trees. It is as I said in the beginning, everyone is in too much of a hurry.'

Monsieur Pamplemousse felt it was time to take a hand. 'If a job is worth doing,' he said, 'it is worth doing well.

'I live near the vineyard of *Clos Montmartre*. It has over 2000 vines; mostly Gamy and Pinot Noir. It is overseen by a Monsieur Gourdin. Every year at the time of the harvest he supervises the taking of the grapes to the *mairie* for fermentation in the basement.'

'That is true,' said the *gendarme*. 'I am told that at such times they can smell it in the *Prefecture de Police* next door. It is a good smell and it reminds them to get ready for the big street party on the first Saturday in October – the *Fête des Vendages*.'

'Unfortunately,' continued Monsieur Pamplemousse, 'because the vines are planted on a North facing slope, even in a good summer it is hard to produce top quality wine. It used to be said that the 700 or so bottles they manage to produce acted as a diuretic, every quart becoming four more, making those who drank it leap around like goats. But it is all in a good cause. The money from the sale

18

goes to charity. For many years it was the only vineyard left in Paris to keep the flag flying. Since his arrival, Monsieur Goudin has inspired others. Small vineyards are starting to spring up all over the place.'

'That is also true,' agreed the *gendarme*. 'Once upon a time the Paris region had over 20,000 hectares of vineyards, but they were all decimated by the outbreak of *phylloxera* in the late nineteenth century. Now, they are even growing grapes at a fire station in the 9th.'

'In my small way,' continued Monsieur Pamplemousse, 'I help to keep the flag flying. On the balcony of my apartment I have six window boxes. I use them to grow herbs in.'

The *gendarme* looked at him with renewed respect. 'You are to be congratulated, *Monsieur*. There is hope for France yet.'

'You are from the Auvergne?' suggested the Peugeot owner.

Monsieur Pamplemousse confessed that he was.

'I thought as much. With respect, I detect a streak of stubbornness. Also the interest in food.'

'Auvergnats play an integral part in the history of Paris brasseries,' agreed the latest arrival. He turned to Monsieur Pamplemousse. 'Have we not met somewhere before?'

'I think not,' said Monsieur Pamplemousse.

'I never forget a face,' said the man. He stared at the figure hunched in the passenger seat. 'The dog, too. He looks very familiar.'

Pommes Frites gazed back at him unblinkingly.

'He is much the same way,' said Monsieur Pamplemousse pointedly. 'He never forgets a face either, and I see no signs of recognition.'

'Once you've seen one Afghan, you've seen the lot,' said

19

the Peugeot owner. Unclipping his pen the interviewer made another entry on his form.

'Afghan?' repeated Monsieur Pamplemousse. He avoided catching Pommes Frites' eye again for fear of what he might see. There were certain key words that met with instant disapproval. Afghan was probably one of them.

'He is a Bloodhound.'

The man gave a shrug. 'Ah, well. Be that as it may. It is just that you sound as though you have a professional interest in food, *Monsieur*, and I happen to be in the business.'

Monsieur Pamplemousse gave a non-committal reply. If he said he worked for *Le Guide*, the oldest and most respected gastronomic bible in all France, the floodgates would open. Given the combined interest in food of his present company, he would never get away.

'I merely mention it because I happen to have a ticket for the Claude Chavignol show tomorrow evening,' said the man. 'His new series has just started. *Monsieur* will know him, of course. Now, there is a cook for you.'

'I know *of* him,' said Monsieur Pamplemousse guardedly. 'In fact, I often pass the studios where the programme is made. They are not far from where I live...'

'Then it must be meant.' The man felt inside his jacket and withdrew a strip of pasteboard.

'Here. It is a shame to waste it. My brother gave it to me. He knows someone who works there. I'm sorry it is for one person only but I shall be away, so I am unable to make use of it.'

Monsieur Pamplemousse hesitated. He had no wish to hurt the other's feelings, but the programme went out on Monday evenings and if he watched television at all he opted for CANAL +, where there was often a good film on. Also, according to all the rumours he'd heard, Claude

Chavignol, noted gastronome and television personality, didn't actually know one end of a carrot from the other. One of his colleagues, Bernard, who also knew someone who worked on the show – a cousin twice removed who was a cameraman – maintained that a minion actually made an incision along the length of any root vegetables so that Monsieur Chavignol would know exactly where he should place his implement.

'Have you noticed that part is never shown in close-up?' Bernard had been only too anxious to air his inside knowledge. 'They always cut away to a shot of the audience. Even then they have a nurse standing by in case the knife slips.'

'Now you mention it,' the man from the census broke into his thoughts. 'I have a feeling I've seen you somewhere before too... I have been racking my brains...'

Monsieur Pamplemousse crossed himself *'Treize, douze, onze, dix, neuf, huit, sept, six, cinq, quatre, trois, deux, un...'* he said, anxious to change the subject.

'Are you all right, *Monsieur*?' asked the official.

Removing his hat, Monsieur Pamplemousse bowed in the direction of the man's hut before replying. 'I thought I saw a magpie perched on the roof. Where I come from to see one magpie is considered bad luck. It is worse than crossed knives. Reciting the numbers one to thirteen quickly in reverse order is a kind of talisman. My mother, God rest her soul, always swore by it. And she lived to a ripe old age.'

'I can't see it,' said the man.

'There you are!' said Monsieur Pamplemousse. 'Already it has taken fright.'

'They are solitary birds,' the *gendarme* broke in. 'All the same, I agree it is not a good sign. The magpie is said to be a hybrid of the raven and the dove, which means that when Noah released those two birds from the ark, the magpie itself was never baptized in the waters of the flood.'

'It is not a happy bird,' agreed the Peugeot driver. 'If a single magpie croaks near a house it is said that one of the occupants will die.' He gave a chuckle as he looked at the interviewer. 'I wouldn't fancy having your job.'

Hearing a veritable symphony of protesting horns from further down the road, the *gendarme* terminated the conversation.

He saluted. *'Pardon, Messieurs...'*

From the expression on his face as he set off towards the line of cars, he was about to throw the book at their owners. The prospects for getting away in a hurry didn't look good. Excessive exhaust fumes would be noted. The depth of tyre treads measured. Papers checked.

'It is very kind of you. It so happens I am starting a week's holiday...'

Accepting the ticket as a means of making good his own escape, Monsieur Pamplemousse slipped it into an inside pocket next to his wallet and tendered his goodbyes. After handshakes all round and with sympathetic cries of *'bonne chance'* ringing in his ears, he resumed his journey.

Glancing in the rear view mirror before pulling out he derived a certain amount of satisfaction when he saw the official, having set off towards his hut, pause to gaze up at the sky as though having second thoughts.

Looking back over his shoulder, Pommes Frites saw what was happening too and clearly felt the same way.

The possibility that in the days to come there would be many worse matters to occupy their respective minds didn't occur to either of them. Pommes Frites fell into a state of gloom at the prospect of having cold left-over tripe for his lunch. As for Monsieur Pamplemousse, his mind was on other things.

Once round the first corner, he put his foot down on the accelerator pedal.

So much for taking a short cut in order to save time. He still had fifty or so kilometres to go. On a good day it could take the best part of an hour. On a bad Sunday there was no telling...

That was another thing about Agathe – she didn't take kindly to people being late. Especially after she had been slaving away over a hot stove. And her with her bad back!

Chapter Two

Monsieur Pamplemousse might have forgotten all about the ticket if Doucette hadn't come across an item in *Le Parisien* next morning at breakfast.

She was about to go through the list of planned *manifestations* for the day – a procession of striking street cleaners in Passy, another involving veterinary surgeons in the Place de la Bastille – when her eye fastened on a piece of traffic news.

'I see now why you were so late yesterday, Aristide,' she said. 'Fancy! A five kilometre tail-back at Porte de Bercy! I must phone Agathe and tell her it wasn't entirely your fault.'

'I doubt if she will believe you,' said Monsieur Pamplemousse, reaching for a second *croissant*. He resisted the temptation to add that her sister was also partly responsible. As with her *tripes à la mode de Caen*, it wouldn't go down well. He produced the ticket instead, and immediately wished he hadn't.

'Of course you must go!' said Doucette. 'They're always showing shots of the audience and I haven't seen you on television for ages. Not since your days with the *Sûreté* when you were working on a difficult case. You may even get invited to take part.'

Monsieur Pamplemousse looked dubious. 'Not if I can help it,' he said.

'Think of Pommes Frites,' replied Doucette. 'He has never seen you on the screen.'

'I doubt if he ever will,' said Monsieur Pamplemousse obstinately. 'Dogs don't have the benefit of persistency of vision. I shall be just a blur like everything else...'

'Don't you be so sure,' said Doucette darkly. 'Pommes Frites sees what he wants to see.'

She was right, of course. Who was to say for certain what dogs could or could not see? They had their own methods. Anyway, there were times when it was best not to argue.

Which was why that same evening found him in the *Centre de Télévision et Ciné de la Butte* watching a studio clock tick away the final seconds before *Cuisine de Chavignol* resumed following a break for a filmed item.

Arriving at the last possible moment, hoping for a seat at the back of the audience so that he could make a quick getaway, his plan had misfired. It was a case of the last shall be first and he was ushered into the front row.

Worse still, much worse, although he had no doubt Doucette would be pleased for Pommes Frites' sake, it meant he could be in line to join the select few Claude Chavignol chose to join him at table for the finale: *Dîner avec Chavignol*.

The possibility that long before the evening was over he would have a much more pressing reason for being on stage anyway didn't enter his mind.

Had he been recognised when he took his seat? He felt sure the answer was "yes". He'd caught a glimpse of the great man in the wings, weighing up the pros and cons of his potential guests. Their eyes had met momentarily. Lips pursed, the host held Monsieur Pamplemousse's gaze for what felt like an unnecessarily long time, as though filing his presence away in the back of his mind for some reason.

Watching the programme at home, it had always seemed to Monsieur Pamplemousse that Claude Chavignol derived an inordinate amount of pleasure in embarrassing the participants and he had no wish to become one of his victims.

Doucette, who didn't trust men with fleshy lips, was very down to earth on the subject, maintaining he should never have shaved off his moustache.

Since she didn't like men with beards either, believing it meant they had something to hide, Monsieur Pamplemousse was tempted to say she couldn't have it both ways. It was like giving a man two ties for Christmas and as soon he tried one on, asking what was wrong with the other.

As usual, she had the last word. What was it she had said?

"If you stuck a pin in that man's ego he would flutter around the room like a pricked balloon before finally disappearing up his own *derrière*."

Monsieur Pamplemousse had pretended to be mildly shocked at the time. It was unlike her to be quite so censorious, or so earthy.

Although it was his first visit to the studios, he had often caught glimpses of them from the outside when he and Pommes Frites were out for a walk. Situated not far from where they lived, but further down the hill towards the Boulevard de Clichy, it was one of those half-hidden enclaves peculiar to Montmartre. Often bigger than they looked, sometimes put to good use and thriving with activity, as was the present case, but more often than not monuments to a bygone age following years of neglect.

Occasionally he stopped to peer between the wrought iron bars of some electrically operated gates that opened on to a courtyard surrounded on all four sides by ancient buildings. Windows, which at one time had been like eyeless holes in the walls, now sported gleaming white shutters, although he strongly suspected many of the openings behind them were bricked up, concealing the fact that the inside had been gutted. Beneath each shutter there was a window box full of carefully tended flowers.

The courtyard was usually full of parked cars, often including an old Facel Vega Excellence in immaculate condition. In its time it had been France's answer to Britain's Rolls Royce and Germany's Mercedes-Benz, and he took it to belong to Monsieur Chavignol himself, since it was very much a Show Biz car, beloved of American film stars: Ava Gardner, Tony Curtis and Danny Kaye to name but a few, and was always in a special marked area by the main entrance to the studios.

More than once he had seen people queuing for audience shows, never dreaming that one day he would be joining them.

Rumour had it that Chavignol had purchased the site for a song. If that were true, his investment had certainly paid off. It was a case of money making money. Having converted the buildings into a complex of studios at a time when everyone seemed to be going independent, he had never looked back; least of all – again, so it was said – at those whose toes he had trodden on during his progress up the ladder of fame.

His own weekly show, which took place in a simulated theatre with a fake proscenium arch and raked seating for an audience of around 150, followed a set pattern. Fifty minutes of something borrowed, something blue, something old and something new: chat show, game show, the occasional musical item, a touch of magic here and there, plus various cookery items, all rolled into one.

Cynics who took the view that you can never underestimate the public's taste must have had their fears confirmed, for in many respects it was a combination of all that was worst in television. That said, it was compulsive viewing and regularly topped the charts.

Host, anchorman, magician, raconteur, wit; once Claude Chavignol got going, *bons mots* culled by his team of researchers flowed in a never-ending stream via the autocue.

"In this world there are only two tragedies. One is not getting what one wants, the other is getting it."

"Nothing that is worth knowing can be taught."

Oscar Wilde might well have consulted his copyright lawyer had he been alive to hear them.

Marcel Aymé (1902-1967) would have joined in. Monsieur Pamplemousse recognised "life always comes to a bad end" as being a quotation from one of his more bizarre works for the simple reason that a bronze statue based on his book *The Man Who Could Pass Through Walls* protruded from a wall outside their apartment block. Pommes Frites had left his mark on it many a time.

Oozing insincerity from every pore, master of all he surveyed, the term "television personality" fitted the programme's host much like his immaculately tailored, dark blue, buttoned up to the neck, Nehru suit.

Seeing him in the flesh for the first time, Monsieur Pamplemousse realised that in one respect at least the description "manufactured" did him an injustice, for his hands were long and slender and beautifully manicured. They were a magician's hands.

All that apart, he certainly wouldn't have wanted to work for him. Those under him probably led a dog's life. It showed in his choice of warm-up artiste: a little-known comedian who was good, but not so good that he would take the shine off the host. After the first few jokes he had set about drilling the audience in the part they had to play. First the length and volume of their applause, then their enthusiastic echoing of "YUMS" – a word used by the host whenever he tasted one of his own dishes.

So far, the programme had been par for the course.

First, the reminiscing about his childhood: helping in the kitchen. 'There is nothing like the taste of raw cake mix – scraping out the mixing bowl – licking the spoon clean...' A chorus of "YUMS" rang round the studio.

Feigning being worn out by it all, Monsieur Chavignol filled a glass jug with water from a tap, took a Paris goblet and poured out a glass of red wine.

Monsieur Pamplemousse wondered what his colleague, Glandier, would have to say about it. Born and brought up in the Savoy mountains, Glandier had often been snowed up for weeks on end and he had an extensive repertoire of tricks he'd perfected as a child.

'One of the oldest in the book.' Monsieur Pamplemousse could hear his voice. 'First lace the water jug with some ferric ammonium sulphate, then make sure the bottom of the glass contains a similar amount of sodium salicylate. Add water, and Hey Presto – red wine! There's nothing to it.'

All the same, performed with practised style, as it had been on this occasion, it never failed.

The hot tip of the week: what to do if a *sauce Béarnaise* goes wrong – had followed.

'Never add warm water to a warm sauce. Add luke-warm water if the *béarnaise* is cold. Add cold water if it is tepid...'

Brief and to the point, the filmed insert only lasted a couple of minutes, but during that time a group of scene hands invaded the kitchen area, assembled a cabinet the size of a telephone kiosk, placed it in position on a pre-marked spot, then vanished as fast as they had come. It was practically poetry in motion.

Their place was taken by a scantily clad girl – extremely small, and more flesh than sequins. Having attached a large round clock to a lighting stand, she made sure all three hands were set to 12.00 o'clock, then turned it to face the audience.

During that time Chavignol had changed into a regular two-piece suit. With it he wore a Hermès tie that looked as though it been specially designed, for it converted the maker's horseshoe motif into the double interlocking C logo of the television company. If that were the case it must have cost a bomb.

Brief was not something that could be said for the interview that followed. Having introduced the guest celebrity, Mademoiselle Martine Odette, owner of a chain of health food shops, Monsieur Chavignol had his work cut out getting a word in edgewise. Mounting what was clearly a favourite hobby horse, she launched into an attack on the tyranny of supermarket uniformity, at the same time unashamedly ploughing a well-worn furrow in praise of her own establishments.

'... each time you enter a *Supermarché* and buy a packet of genetically modified, chemically adulterated, irradiated food fed by white-clad operatives into some giant machine in the middle of nowhere before being spewed out into plastic containers containing exact pre-set portions, you are guilty of dumbing down not only yourself, but your children too.'

Cued by the floor manager – soft-soled suede shoes, combat trousers – a kind of uniform in which the common thread was a dark blue tee shirt, again with the company logo emblazoned on the front in gold lettering – the audience dutifully signalled their approval.

'You are also guilty of knocking another nail in the coffin of what makes French cuisine so special,' continued Mademoiselle Odette, 'the freshness of its ingredients and the livelihood of small farmers who grow food not simply for money but out of love for their work... It is a matter of going back to basics...'

Once she had the bit between her snow-white teeth there was no stopping her.

Monsieur Pamplemousse found his attention drawn towards the girl who had brought the clock on. She was now quietly busying herself in the kitchen. Having filled three glasses with water, she half-filled a saucepan, placed it on the stove, and applied a match to the burner.

Hardly rising much above the level of the hotplate, she was what Guilot, another of his colleagues, would have called "a pretty little thing". Guilot invariably added a gloomy rider to the effect that the pretty little things of today often turned into the viragos of tomorrow. No one had ever met his wife, but everyone suspected he spoke from bitter experience, especially as he listed hiking as his favourite pastime.

Consulting a clipboard with the script and running-order typed out on yellow paper, the floor manager began to look anxious as first his circular wind-up signals, then his throat-cutting signs were ignored. He tried tapping his wrist watch.

Monsieur Pamplemousse glanced over his shoulder towards the long window of a production gallery in the wall at the back of the studio. Behind it he could see a glow from a row of monitors. Someone was on their feet looking through the window at the studio floor below. He could guess what was being said. The air would be blue.

It was left to others to do the dirty work. Hand outstretched, Claude Chavignol rose from the settee, terminating the interview in no uncertain manner.

As a call boy escorted Mademoiselle Odette off the set, he crossed over to the kitchen area. If he was thrown by the slight contretemps it didn't show.

A remotely controlled overhead camera on rails tracked in from a wide shot of the studio over the heads of the audience, panned down to the cooking area, then zoomed in to a closer shot as the host entered. At the same time other manned cameras moved in and took up their working positions.

'On the subject of going back to basics...' Having first checked that all was ready, Monsieur Chavignol gave a nod of approval, ushered the girl towards the portable cabinet and opened the door.

As she disappeared into inky blackness he essayed a quick pat on her *derrière*. She gave a squeal. 'Mind you don't get too near any hot fat, *chérie*,' he advised.

This time the laughter was spontaneous.

Closing the door behind her, he turned a key in the lock, returned to the working area and picked up a small tray which he held up towards the nearest camera. A red light came on and a picture of three eggs appeared on the monitors.

'...there is nothing else in the world as basic as an egg, or as useful. Full of protein... rich in vitamins... an egg is a meal in itself, and yet... *Alors!* Hands up all those in the audience who can say, hand on their heart, they are able to prepare a perfectly boiled egg... every time.'

There was a noticeable lack of response.

'The simplest things,' continued Monsieur Chavignol, '...a steak... *pommes frites*...a toasted *baguette*, are often the hardest to perfect. Some people even have trouble boiling a kettle of water. But, perhaps because it is impossible to see inside it, boiling an egg can be the most hit-and-miss affair of all.'

While he was talking, Monsieur Chavignol adjusted the heat under the saucepan. Another camera craned higher for a close-up of the water. It was just beginning to simmer.

33

'Now, the very first thing to establish is the age of the egg. The three I have here are all different. I have no idea which is which. All I know is they were taken out of the refrigerator at least half an hour ago.

'One is old, one is newly laid, and one somewhere in between, perhaps three or four days old. That is the one I am looking for. How do I know which is which? The answer is simple!'

Placing each egg in a separate glass of water, he stood back. The studio monitors began showing a series of close ups.

'As you see, in the first glass the egg is lying horizontally across the bottom. That shows it is newly laid – too fresh for my purpose. In the second, the egg has settled vertically. That means it is stale. Therefore I shall choose the third one, which is slightly tilted on its base, indicating it is only a few days old.

'Since I like my eggs soft boiled, not too soft, but with the white just set, I shall allow it six minutes. The water, as you saw, is simmering, but not boiling. If you wish, at this point you can make a hole in the egg with a needle or a mapping pin to let out any air. That will prevent the shell cracking.

'I take a spoon and lower it gently into the water... like so... Now!' Releasing the egg Monsieur Chavignol turned and set the clock in motion.

The studio was so quiet the sound of ticking could be plainly heard, but almost immediately it was drowned by a loud knocking from inside the cabinet. Giving an impatient wave, he turned his back on the audience and began searching through his pockets for the key. The seconds went by and it was over a minute before panic clearly began to set in. All the while the banging grew louder.

Abandoning his search at long last, he signalled to the

floor manager, who ran off the set, returning moments later with the scene crew. Three minutes had passed and the banging now had a desperate quality to it. Monsieur Pamplemousse could feel the tension communicating itself to the audience, running through it like a bush fire. A staff nurse and a fireman appeared in the wings.

The scene men hastily began dismantling the cupboard. Two to each of the four sides, they had it apart in less than a minute, carrying the sections off between them as though they were a series of stretchers.

A gasp went round the audience as they realised the girl had vanished. Once again he could hear Glandier's voice. 'Any girl who allows herself to be sawn in two for real is asking for trouble. The one thing you know for sure when she disappears, gets a circular saw through her torso, or starts to float in mid air, is that it isn't actually happening. If you could see the joins it wouldn't be a very good trick.'

A second wave of panic set in as the audience began to realise that five minutes had gone by and the sweep second hand of the clock had begun its final round.

Several people began calling out words of warning.

Monsieur Chavignol, who was upstage of the clock, unable to see its face, looked round enquiringly, as though wondering what all the fuss was about.

He ambled slowly across to the stove, and without even bothering to check with his watch, looked over his shoulder again. Then, at exactly the right moment, just as the second hand reached the figure twelve, he removed the egg from the saucepan with a flourish.

A gasp of relief went round the audience.

What followed was a foregone conclusion. Placing the egg in a holder, he had no sooner finished removing the top with knife, than a piece of lightly browned bread flew out of a toaster. Catching it expertly with his left hand, he dipped a teaspoon into the egg with his right, and Hey Presto – it was "YUMS" time again.

No doubt Glandier would have had his own views on the matter, but to the studio audience it was a *tour de force* and they showed their appreciation in no uncertain manner as Monsieur Chavignol dabbed at his mouth with a napkin and left the stage.

A filmed insert on the demise of the bee that followed was something of an anticlimax.

It seemed that in certain parts of France, Limousin in particular, apiarists were having a bad time. In gathering nectar and pollen, the bees were also imbibing a chemical called *imidacloprid* which caused them to lose their sense of direction, rendering them incapable of finding their way home.

Monsieur Pamplemousse knew how they must feel. His journey back from Melun had been even worse than it was going. With hold-ups everywhere, he had ended up getting lost in the 14th *arrondissement* of all places. Not that he had admitted it to Doucette, whose only comment as they went round the Place Victor Basch for the third time had been 'Everywhere is beginning to look exactly the same!'

From his vantage point in the front row he could see Monsieur Chavignol, his immaculately tailored suit now replaced by chef's whites, hovering behind a flat awaiting his cue.

Truth to tell, he had been enjoying himself more than he'd expected. Like him or loathe him, it was hard not to admire the sheer professionalism of someone who was able to hold an audience so completely in the palm of his hand.

As the narrator's voice – recorded on film and relayed to the audience via studio fold-back – reached the final summing up, an assistant hurried onto the set carrying a loaded tray.

Instead of the usual *mise en place* board with its mixture of prepared ingredients – chopped nuts, herbs, butter – all the time-consuming items appropriate to the job in hand, there was a single large mound covered by a white cloth. A second assistant followed on behind carrying an ice-bucket and stand which he placed out of vision behind the kitchen counter.

Standing alongside Monsieur Chavignol, the floor manager waited with his arm raised, ready to cue him. As the film came to an end he converted the movement into a signal for applause.

Taking his place behind the counter, Claude Chavignol acknowledged the reception with a bow.

'Tonight,' he announced, 'I have decided not to hold my usual dinner party.' Monsieur Pamplemousse breathed a sigh of relief. 'Instead, I want to tell you about a friend – a very old, a very dear friend...'

Heaving his huge bulk on to a stool, Monsieur Chavignol went into serious mode. As the background lights were dimmed he leaned across the counter to address the nearest camera.

'This friend of mine was born and brought up on the west coast of France, in a small town not far from Bordeaux.

'They say it is a wise child who knows his own father, but my friend never knew his parents. They were taken from him soon after he was born.

'Nevertheless, despite the loss, in many ways he enjoyed an idyllic childhood. The sandy beaches in the area were his playground, and during the summer months the warm sea his to laze in. In the circumstances it wasn't surprising that as he grew older he began to lead the life of a beachcomber, a drifter...' Monsieur Chavignol paused while suitable stock material appeared on the screen: pictures of a beach, people bathing, a sunset...

'I doubt if he ever strayed more than five miles from the spot where he was born,' he continued. 'However, life wasn't all play, and as time went by the inevitable happened. Mixing with others of his kind, he began to drink. At first only in a minor way, but gradually his liquid consumption grew and grew until it reached a truly awesome rate. He thought nothing of downing on average a litre an hour. And that was only the beginning. One litre became two, then three, then four or more. There was no stopping him. It was life on the tiles with a vengeance. There were those who equated his daily consumption with that of a swimming pool.'

A murmur went round the studio audience and a lady sitting near Monsieur Pamplemousse clucked disapprovingly.

'All day and every day, he could be found seated at the bar, and there he would remain, staring into space as though he had become part of the fixtures and fittings, cocooned against the outside world with all its problems.

'Then suddenly – as current phraseology has it – he "came out". It was almost as though he had thought it all through and decided he had grown tired of being a man. Overnight, and with never a backward glance, he underwent a sex change.

'Worse still, not long afterwards, almost as though the experience had given him some kind of inner confidence, he reverted to his former persuasion.

'Indeed, he went through a period of being quite literally all at sea; a genuine hermaphrodite, not knowing which way to go.

'As a man, his rough exterior concealed a heart of gold. As a girl he was extraordinarily seductive.

38

'Some might say he enjoyed the best of both worlds; others that he endured the worst of each, for he was not without his enemies.

'Reflecting on the life of my dear friend, perhaps it was all for the best that this state of affairs wasn't allowed to continue.

'Before attaining what we would call his majority, he – or perhaps it was she at the time – received a summons from the great table in the sky.

'Soon afterwards the bulldozers moved in. They destroyed his home, grinding it down as though it had never existed. Where did it end up? Who knows? Quite possibly to help form the base for some new road project.'

Reaching for the ice bucket, Claude Chavignol produced a bottle and began removing the foil top.

'Tonight, I want you to join me in drinking a toast. In many parts of France the choice would be a white wine, a Chablis perhaps, or a Riesling. In Ireland it would be a drink known as Guinness. In America, and perhaps in Australia or New Zealand, it would be a Chardonnay. But always, when I think of my absent friend, I think of Champagne. For me, the two go together. I see it as a marriage made in heaven.'

Monsieur Chavignol paused to allow shots of studio assistants arriving at the end of each row, handing out glasses of champagne to an appreciative audience. While that was happening, an assistant floor manager dashed on to the set again and changed the bottle for an already opened one.

'For once,' Monsieur Chavignol began filling his own glass, 'I am not going to the oven to produce the "one I made earlier"...'

He gave a mock bow as someone clapped nervously and a titter went round the audience.

'Instead...' Slipping off the stool he crossed to the tray and with a practised flourish removed the cloth, to reveal a metal stand. Below it there was a small plate of thinly-sliced dark brown bread, a dish of butter, half a lemon, a three-pronged fork, and a short stainless steel knife with a guard and maplewood handle.

Resting on top of the stand was a larger plate piled high with seaweed. On top of that, nestling in a bed of crushed ice, lay a single oyster in its shell.

Allowing a couple of beats to establish the shot, Monsieur Chavignol took the shell in his left hand. Holding it flat side uppermost, he picked up the knife, slipped the pointed end into the "hinged" section, moving it horizontally at the same time in order to sever the ligament, and with a quick twist of his wrist prised the two sides apart.

Leaving the oyster in the bottom half of the shell, he returned it to its original resting place. At the same time a camera zoomed slowly in to a tight close-up.

Filling the screen as it did, the picture with its mixture of colours; the yellow of the lemon, the dark green of the seaweed, the many greys of the oyster nestling inside the shell with its lustrous combination of almost translucent calcium white and mother of pearl, gave it the appearance of a still life by some early Dutch master, and the audience duly applauded.

'As you will have doubtless guessed,' said Monsieur Chavignol, seen now in a wider shot, 'my friend was a mollusc.' (A murmur from the audience suggested that many of them *hadn't* made the connection). 'To give him... her... *its* full name: a *spéciale fine de claire*.

'And why is it so special? Because during its lifetime this small *crassottrea angulata*, born near the Île d'Oleron on the Charente coast of France, survived all that nature

40

could throw at it: storms, parasites, the ravages of a creature known as the boring sponge, barnacles, the slipper limpet, the dog whelk, crabs, octopus and other fish in search of food; the starfish, a creature that can wrap its arms around its prey and with its powerful suckers pull the shell apart before devouring the contents.'

He removed the shell and held it up to the light.

'This one – a *numero deux* if I am any judge of size – will have lived for some three years before being taken from the hollow tile where it had made its home and placed in a *claire*, a shallow pool of water in an area once used for the production of salt. It is *spéciale* because it was privileged to remain there to fatten for eight weeks instead of the more usual four, and during that time share it with only nine others to the square metre instead of being one of a vast crowd.

'As a female, in its time it must have spawned hundreds of millions of eggs; as a male it would have had the perhaps even more onerous task of trying to fertilize as many of them as possible before other creatures gobbled them up.

'As soon as the eight weeks had passed it was removed from the *claire* in order to meet its greatest enemy of all – *Homo Sapiens*.'

Reaching for the fork, Monsieur Chavignol plunged the sharply pointed tines inside the shell. Tilting back his head, he turned and presented his profile in silhouette to the audience.

'As the Irish writer Jonathan Swift once said: "He was a bold man that first ate an oyster", but I must say I am very glad he did. Otherwise we might never have known the exquisite pleasure which is theirs to give.

'Sad to relate...' opening his mouth, he popped the oyster laden fork inside it, 'my own very dear friend is no longer with us.'

The audience, awaiting their cue, remained silent. But instead of his usual cry of "YUMS", Monsieur Claude Chavignol gave vent to a strangled groan.

Holding his throat, he toppled forward, clutching desperately at the counter with his other hand for support. Unable to retain a grip on the polished surface, he began to slide, and before an invited audience of 150, and countless millions of others unseen, slowly disappeared from view.

Monsieur Pamplemousse's first reaction was that it was yet another of his tricks, albeit a somewhat macabre one, and for a second or two he sat where he was. Even the floor manager seemed taken by surprise. Cupping his hands over his headset, he was clearly listening to reactions from the gallery. The nurse was speaking into her mobile.

Less than half a kilometre away, Pommes Frites sat staring at the Pamplemousses' television screen. On the whole he liked cookery programmes. It didn't require much in the way of persistency of vision to recognise a close-up of a sausage when he saw one, and although molluscs didn't figure large in his list of favourite comestibles, he'd had no difficulty with Monsieur Chavignol's oyster.

What he hadn't bargained on was seeing his master suddenly appear in the picture. Bending down behind the desk he dragged the man in the white coat to his feet. Standing behind him, he joined his own hands together to form a fist and having placed it low down on the man's stomach, thrust it sharply upwards.

Just as things were beginning to get interesting, the screen went blank.

'It isn't a bit of good doing that,' said Madame Pamplemousse, as Pommes Frites disappeared behind the television set. 'That won't bring the picture back. And if you ask me,' she added, 'that goes for Monsieur Chavignol as well!'

Further down the slopes of the Butte Montmartre, Monsieur Pamplemousse also looked round in vain. Having apparently got nowhere with the Heimlich Manoeuvre, things were getting desperate. The seconds were ticking away. Assuming Chavignol was choking on the oyster there was approximately four minutes from start to finish before unconsciousness set in, followed by possible brain damage and death.

Turning the victim round to face him, Monsieur Pamplemousse hesitated. Mindful of Doucette's earlier remarks on the subject of lips, it was easy to see why no one else was exactly fighting to be the first to administer the kiss of life.

He included himself in that, but with more reason than most. The aptness of Marcel Aymé's words: "Life always comes to a bad end", was all too apparent. It didn't need Pommes Frites' olfactory powers to detect on the other's breath the faint but all too familiar odour of bitter almonds.

In his book that meant only one thing: cyanide!

Chapter Three

'Aristide... what an awful thing to happen!'

Doucette must have been listening out for him. As soon as the lift came to a halt on the seventh floor, she opened the door of their apartment and came out to greet him. Pommes Frites followed on behind, wagging his tail in silent admiration.

'You saw it all?'

The truth was Monsieur Pamplemousse had no idea how much of the *catastrophe* had gone out. At the time he'd had too many other things on his mind to notice whether the programme was still on the air or not. From what Doucette said, it sounded as though he had beaten the vision mixer to the draw in one of those moments when a second or two can seem like an eternity. Perhaps those up in the gallery had also been wondering whether the whole thing was for real or not. It was one of the perils of live television.

'You were on for quite a long time. We both felt very proud of you. Pommes Frites was most upset when they faded the programme. It's a pity you didn't have your hair cut like I told you to...'

Doucette clearly had a lot bottled up.

'There were more important things going on,' said Monsieur Pamplemousse pointedly. 'I doubt if anyone noticed.'

'He *will* be all right?'

Closing the apartment door behind him, Monsieur Pamplemousse shrugged himself out of his overcoat and hung it in the hall cupboard.

'I doubt if any insurance company would issue a policy on his behalf. They wouldn't fancy his chances.'

Looking for his slippers he realised Pommes Frites, anticipating his every wish as usual, was already waiting guard over them by the armchair near the window in the next room.

'But how awful for you. Was it his heart do you think?'

Monsieur Pamplemousse made a face. 'Everyone dies of heart failure, Couscous. Sometimes it is brought on by old age... sometimes it is helped on its way...'

'You don't mean? But that is terrible...' Madame Pamplemousse followed him into the living room.

'When you were late back I assumed you had accompanied Monsieur Chavignol to the hospital.'

The chance would have been a fine thing. As soon as the nurse came off the telephone she went into action, taking over from him, issuing orders right left and centre. Speaking for himself he would have left Monsieur Chavignol where he was, rustling up some screens to protect him from the gaze of the audience until help arrived. Instead, the same burly scene hands who erected the cabinet had carried him off somewhere behind the scenes.

His own doctor was like that. He always made himself scarce when he saw an accident. 'Don't touch,' was his motto. 'Leave it to the experts – *les Sapeurs-Pompiers*.' It sounded like good advice.

Leaving it to the experts, but feeling a bit shut out of things all the same, Monsieur Pamplemousse had accepted the perfunctory thanks of the studio manager and joined the rest of the audience as they filed silently out of the studio. It occurred to him that someone might have asked if there was a doctor in the house, but he kept his counsel. He had already done more than his bit.

Once outside, instead of taking a short cut up the Rue

Tholozé towards the Moulin de la Galette, he opted for the gentler climb leading towards the Place des Abbesses. It was hard making the transition from the bright lights to the gloom of the evening and he needed time to think.

He hadn't gone far before he heard the sound of approaching sirens behind him; what sounded like the *Sapeurs-Pompiers* – first on the scene as usual, then an ambulance – probably from the Hôpital Bichat Claude Bernard near the *Périphérique*, then a police car. All three stopped together, further away than he expected. Perhaps they were caught up in the evening traffic.

Feeling in his pocket he wondered then, as he was wondering now, if he had done the right thing. "Tampering with evidence" was what some of his old colleagues back at the Quai des Orfèvres might have called it. "Typical Pamplemousse. He's always been a bit of a loner," others might have said. Perhaps he should have insisted on staying put until the Police arrived. Pulled a bit of rank – or ex-rank. The truth of the matter was, he didn't necessarily trust the locals.

Also, seeing the speed at which everyone in the television studios went about their work, if he hadn't acted when he did the objects in his handkerchief could well have been swept up with the rest of the rubbish.

As with taking a short cut on the way to Melun it had been a spur of the moment decision. He told himself that he would hand them in later and make his peace at the same time. Maybe after he'd had something eat.

'I hope you don't mind, Aristide.' Doucette broke into his thoughts. 'I've got you some oysters for *dîner*. I thought it would be a treat.'

'Thank you, Couscous,' said Monsieur Pamplemousse drily. 'It is just what I fancy. A dozen, I hope.'

'Two dozen,' said Madame Pamplemousse nervously. 'I

told you it was a treat. They are your favourite – *spéciale fine de claire*.'

'*Numero deux*?'

'Of course.'

'It gets better and better. Don't worry. It would take more than this evening's little debacle to put me off.'

Nevertheless, he viewed the prospect with rather less relish than usual. Inevitably it was another reminder of his time in the *Sûreté*. In those days, if ever a case took place in a hospital – someone stabbed in the heart, perhaps, or in the kidneys, as happened with the ward sister who had disembowelled one of her patients in the dead of night, a *crime passionelle*, so she had got off comparatively lightly, although it put paid to her prospects of promotion for quite a while – a meal afterwards with those closely involved always seemed to involve eating a dish high-lighting the relevant organ: braised hearts perhaps, or foie *gras de canard*. In those days it hadn't been coincidence. It was the medics' idea of a joke.

'I have some of your favourite *fromage* as well.' Doucette's voice came from the kitchen. 'Saint Agur.'

Monsieur Pamplemousse felt his taste buds begin to salivate. Oysters, blue cheese from the Auvergne – the land of his birth... it had the makings of a classic meal. He might suggest it during the next staff get-together when, sooner or later in the evening, they played a game called "My last meal on earth." Tastes changed over the years, and nowadays he would add *foie gras*, which he wouldn't have chosen at one time. Truffles, of course, and the first of the fresh asparagus from the Landes. The last two being seasonal, it would be a job to combine them, but should the gods be smiling on him and stay their hand until the spring, there was a small window at the end of March when both were available...

In the meantime, Doucette was certainly pushing the boat out. Wondering if by chance he had missed some important anniversary, he felt for his diary. 'What are we having for the main course?'

'Ah, there is a bit of a problem.' Her voice came from the direction of the dining-room now. He heard the sound of clinking cutlery.

'Agathe gave me the remains of yesterday's lunch. She's not very keen on it herself. She only does it for your benefit.'

'*Merde!*' Monsieur Pamplemousse leapt to his feet. 'Do we have to?'

Doucette made tutting noises. 'She's bound to ring up later and ask if we enjoyed it.'

'It's a good job Pommes Frites can't answer the phone,' said Monsieur Pamplemousse bluntly. 'She might learn the truth.'

Ever alive to domestic vibrations, Pommes Frites assumed his gloomy expression, then very firmly lay down and closed his eyes.

Left to his own devices, Monsieur Pamplemousse removed the handkerchief from his trouser pocket and began unwrapping the contents. Holding first one half of an oyster shell delicately between thumb and forefinger as though it were a precious jewel, then the other half, he sniffed each in turn.

Over and above the distinctive odour of the sea, he could still detect the smell of almonds.

Pommes Frites opened one eye, then came over to join him.

'*Non!*' said Monsieur Pamplemousse firmly.

Crossing to a bureau, he opened a drawer and took out a plastic sample bag – another souvenir of his time in the force.

It wouldn't do for Pommes Frites to wake up while they were eating and take it into his head that the contents of the handkerchief was a better bet than Agathe's leftover *tripes à la mode de Caen*. He wouldn't blame him, of course.

Help came in the shape of a bottle; a gift from his colleague, Bernard, who had once been in the wine trade. Bernard was something of an expert in Bordeaux, but following the run of bad years along with the hiking up of prices he had moved over to Burgundy and Rhône. André Brunel's Côtes du Rhône Cuvée Sommelongue even mitigated the horrors of the warmed up meal.

Doucette further redeemed herself with a *soufflé* omelette filled with rose petal jam. Three criss-crossing dark brown lines had been made with a hot poker in the sugared top to form the letter A for Aristide.

What more could any man wish for?

The telephone starting ringing shortly before breakfast next day. The first call was from Monsieur Leclercq, Director of *Le Guide*. He was speaking from his car phone. On finding Monsieur Pamplemousse was out for an early morning walk with Pommes Frites, he left a message asking him to report to his office as soon as possible.

Returning from the *boulangerie* in the Rue Caulaincourt, armed with *croissants* for Doucette, *brioche au sucre* for himself, and a *pain au chocolat* for Pommes Frites (a treat for coming to his rescue the night before and surreptitiously helping to finish off the remains of the *tripes*), Monsieur Pamplemousse encountered a member of the press, notebook in hand, waiting for him outside their apartment block.

Having learnt from bitter experience that you crossed swords with the media at your peril, he did his best to parry the questions: 'Yes, it was entirely a matter of chance that he had been at last night's show.'; 'No, he had no connection whatsoever with Claude Chavignol.'; 'No, he had nothing to add ... the reporter knew as much about things as he did.' The double negative went unnoticed.

It was an unexpected and wholly unwelcome intrusion to his life, and the *petit déjeuner* he had been looking forward to suffered accordingly.

Doucette complaining that Pommes Frites had left chocolate stains all over a new rug didn't help, especially when he tried to lick them up and only made matters worse.

Monsieur Pamplemousse sought refuge on the balcony in order to tend his herb garden.

It was something he had come to late in life. From small beginnings – a wooden window box containing parsley and chives, it had grown into a neat row of some half a dozen pottery *jardinières* supported on metal brackets attached to the railings that ran the length of the terrace. Basil now rubbed leaves with lemon thyme – he was particularly proud of his dwarf *Thymus erectus* – which was like a tiny tree, and dwarf green curled parsley shared the same container. Marjoram grew alongside sorrel, and there was tarragon and fennel too.

They were his pride and joy, and if other mean-spirited people who entered the building when he happened to be watering them complained to the *concierge*, they knew what they could do; buy an umbrella! Exposed to the elements as they were, the pots soon dried out and needed constant attention during the summer. Now, with a week at home, it was time to think about carrying out some thinning and dividing up ready for next spring. The remaining basil leaves had to be stripped for drying; and the parsley cut for Doucette's tea – she maintained it was good for her complexion, and it seemed to work.

He might even splash out on some new plants. In fact, had he not been held up that Sunday he'd planned to call in at a nursery on the way to Agathe.

No sooner had he started work than he heard the phone ringing.

'It's Monsieur Leclercq again,' called Doucette. 'He's back in his office. He would like to see you as soon as possible. And will you please bring Pommes Frites?'

Monsieur Pamplemousse grunted a reply. The chives were still doing well. Bernard's advice to deflower them early in the year had paid off. He wasn't surprised at hearing from the Director, but he wondered why Pommes Frites had been summoned too. Not that he was ever made to feel less than welcome, but specific invitations were rare.

The borage seeds he had sown during the summer months were also coming along fine. Who was it said "One is nearer God's heart in a garden than anywhere else on earth?" An Englishman probably, or more likely an English lady poet. He couldn't remember, but if it were true then surely even a humble collection of window boxes must stand him in good stead. The fact that they were on the seventh floor of his apartment block situated on the slopes of the highest point in Paris ought to give him a head start.

'Didn't you hear me call, Aristide?' Doucette appeared in the doorway. 'The phone hasn't stopped ringing.'

'Who is it now?

'That *journal* Claude Chavignol wrote his weekly column for. The editor said he wanted to make you an offer you couldn't refuse.'

'I hope you told him where to go...'

'Certainly not. I asked him what he had in mind.'

'And...?'

'He wants to engage you to find the murderer. Think of it, Aristide. It will be just like old times. While you're doing it you can have free use of the column and all the support you need. And it would mean your being in Paris for a while instead of disappearing for weeks on end eating your way around France. He seemed to think the whole thing was meant.'

There it was again. The same old syndrome; was it coincidence, or was it pre-ordained?

'He said they would pay you well.'

'I know what the Director would say about that...'

'I know something else, Aristide. You're not going to escape that easily. Have you looked outside?'

Glancing over the railings, he recognised the man who had waylaid him earlier. He had been joined by several others. There was no mistaking their calling. It wasn't just the cameras at the ready, it was their attitude, and the way they were dressed. They didn't just stand around; they "lurked", ready to pounce. One even had the effrontery to hang his hat on Marcel Aymé's statue, and was about to take a picture of it. Another, sporting a camera with an enormous narrow angle lens, pointed it straight at the balcony. He hoped he was pleased with the result. At that distance he didn't fancy the man's chances, although you never knew these days; some lenses even had built in stabilizers.

Monsieur Pamplemousse was no stranger to fame. Once upon a time it had been forced on him by a voracious press anxious to fill their pages with an update on the latest crime straight from the horse's mouth.

That had been the downside of the job, although in those days he'd had the weight of the Paris *Sûreté* to back him up. Now, if he took up the offer he would enjoy no such luxury.

'If he rings back tell him I'm out.'

'But, Aristide...'

'It will be true. I have to see Monsieur Leclereq before I do anything else. I'll go out the back way.'

Hearing the phone start to ring again he gave a sigh. 'There's no peace for the wicked.'

'You said it, Aristide,' said Doucette, 'not me.'

When he arrived at *Le Guide*'s headquarters in the Rue Falbert it felt as though he had just returned from the wars, or rowed all the way round the world single-handed. Even old Rambaud, the gatekeeper, broke into a smile. It was a shame he hadn't got his camera with him. He could have recorded the moment for posterity.

Pommes Frites revelled in their new-found glory.

At least Véronique, Monsieur Leclercq's secretary, had the grace to greet him as though nothing unusual had taken place. She simply smiled her usual warm smile as she ushered him into the holy of holies.

As they entered the room the Director turned away from his desk and, having advanced towards Monsieur Pamplemousse, hand outstretched, issued an instruction to Véronique to tell the switchboard they were not under any circumstances to be disturbed for the next hour, and that if she had any important shopping to do, now would be a very good time. It could hardly have been more pointed.

Pommes Frites seemed to sense the slight frost that descended on the room. Having slaked his thirst from a water bowl laid ready on a napkin, he promptly backed off and sat down to await developments.

Monsieur Pamplemousse's own worst fears were realised when he saw the Director's normally immaculate desk littered with newspapers.

54

As for Monsieur Leclercq, worry lines were etched on his face and he looked as though he hadn't slept a wink all night. His first words confirmed it.

'Pamplemousse – at last! I have hardly slept a wink all night!'

One by one he held up the journals. 'MORT À MONT-MARTRE,' he intoned, picking them up at random. 'MYSTÈRE CHAVIGNOL... HOMICIDE À HUITRE... PAMPLEMOUSSE RIDES AGAIN!' (The last from the *New York Herald Tribune*)

'They make unhappy reading, Pamplemousse.'

A feeling of *déjà vu* came over Monsieur Pamplemousse as he found himself staring at variations of his own likeness appearing beneath the banner headlines. Most were flatteringly old.

'At least Le Monde doesn't carry photographs, Monsieur.'

'We must be thankful for such mercies,' said the Director gloomily, 'however small they may be.

'Monday evenings will no longer be the same,' he read. 'Chavignol was a one-off... A professional to his finger-tips... He will be much mourned.' He sounded bitter, which was unlike him.

'This is bad news,' he continued. 'Your identity is now common knowledge, Pamplemousse. Remember our motto. The three A's: *Action, Accord, Anonymat*.'

'With respect, Monsieur, those precepts have not been breached. There is nothing to link me to *Le Guide*. It is my past affiliations the media are interested in, not my present ones. I venture to suggest that even after seeing the photographs many of those in the trade, waiters, restaurateurs, will not recognise me. Memories are short. People have their own problems.'

Monsieur Leclercq looked doubtful. 'You know what

the media are like. Once they start digging into things there is no knowing what they will turn up.'

'I have no secrets to hide, *Monsieur*,' said Monsieur Pamplemousse virtuously. The response seemed to go home. 'Lucky *Le homme* who can say that, hand on heart, Aristide,' said the Director fervently.

'That apart, the whole unsavoury business will do a great deal of harm to the oyster industry. Already there have been complaints from Locmariaquer. Despite there being an "R" in the month, both Le Dôme and La Coupole have reported a falling off in trade.'

It struck Monsieur Pamplemousse that for some reason best known to himself the Director was either clutching at straws, or failing to grasp the nettle. 'It didn't do much for Monsieur Chavignol either,' he added drily.

'There is good in everything, Pamplemousse,' said the Director. 'In Chavignol's case the best you can say is that it is good riddance to bad rubbish.

'The man was a *monstre* of the very worst kind. *Un salaud... une vache...vielle pouffiasse... merdaillon... scélerat...* It is hard to find words to describe him.'

'You are doing very well, *Monsieur*,' ventured Monsieur Pamplemousse.

'Worst of all, Aristide,' continued the Director, 'the man was a charlatan; a disgrace to his chosen profession.'

'With respect, *Monsieur*, the world of catering doesn't exactly enjoy a spotless reputation at the best of times. You have only to read the book written by that American chef, Monsieur Bourdain, to see what I mean. It is on all the bestseller lists. The public loves reading about these things.'

'What chefs get up to within the confines of their own workplace is a matter between themselves and their colleagues,' said the Director. 'Fornication behind the dishwasher is one thing, but when such behaviour and worse spills over into their home life it is another matter.'

'There is a Madame Chavignol?' broke in Monsieur Pamplemousse. 'From all I have heard...'

'There is indeed!' said Monsieur Leclercq grimly.

'*Hélas!*' He sat down heavily in his chair and gazed out of the window. 'It is about Madame Chavignol that I wish to confer with you.'

'But if her husband was all that you say he was, *Monsieur*, then surely...'

'Then surely she must feel relieved. Is that what you were about to say, Aristide?'

'It would seem to follow, *Monsieur*. However, I long ago ceased to wonder about the way people react in times of stress. Human nature is very complex; at times it is wholly unpredictable.'

Monsieur Leclercq came back to earth from wherever he had been.

'Things are not always as they seem, Aristide.' He glanced nervously towards the door leading to the outer office in case Véronique hadn't taken his advice. 'The story I have to tell you is not a pretty one...'

'Is it about an oyster?' asked Monsieur Pamplemousse, seeking to help the Director out.

Monsieur Leclerq stared at him. 'No, Pamplemousse, it is not! It happened a few weeks ago when my wife and I were attending a party at the Chavignol's home in the 7th *arrondissement*.

'It was a warm summer evening and there was a string quartet playing in the garden. I was dancing with the hostess on the patio when I happened to pass some innocent remark about how nice it was to see such a happy couple. I was thinking of her husband, of course, who I must say had been the perfect host; exuding *bonhomie* to all and sundry.

'Madame Chavignol stopped on the spot and looked me straight in the eye. Having suggested we sit the next dance out, she fortified herself with a glass or two of Roederer Crystal champagne.

'At this point I would ask you to bear in mind that there are two sides to every story. I am simply relating the facts of what transpired in chronological order. What she had to tell me made Casanova's memoirs pale by comparison.

'I felt it my duty to console her. She needed a shoulder to cry on. I didn't mention it to Madame Leclercq at the time because for some reason she had taken a violent dislike to our hostess. You know how women can be on such occasions... although in retrospect I have to admit she showed remarkable prescience. As far as I was concerned there was nothing to it, of course...'

Monsieur Pamplemousse raised both hands heaven-wards. 'Of course, *Monsieur*. Not for one moment did I think otherwise.'

'People always tend to think the worst...'

'That has been my experience, too, *Monsieur*.'

'In your case, Pamplemousse,' said the Director sternly, 'not without reason I fear.

'But I ask you this. How would your wife feel if you preferred sleeping with a plastic inflatable nun by your side? How would any normal woman feel?'

'I cannot speak for Doucette, *Monsieur*, although she is such a sound sleeper she would probably never know. As for Madame Chavignol, I have never met the lady, but if her husband was all you say he was, it may well have been a blessing in disguise.'

'It is hard to disguise a plastic inflatable nun, Pamplemousse, and it was not always by his side,' said the Director meaningfully. 'As she told the story to me that evening, he was often astride it. Acting, if you will pardon the expression, like the proverbial village pump. There were times when the poor woman lay in fear and trembling that it might explode at any moment.'

'I sympathise,' said Monsieur Pamplemousse. 'But such devices are remarkably resilient these days. Great strides have been made in the field of plastics. Take, *par exemple*, Pommes Frites' inflatable kennel. There was the time when you sent us to that Health Farm in the Pyrénées-Orientales – Château Morgue. If you remember it turned out to be a haunt of drug smugglers. With the door flap of his kennel sealed and the inside filled with helium, it lifted him and most of *Le Guide's* camera equipment with no trouble at all. And that at a time when he also needed to lose weight. Had I not attached a stout line we might never have seen him again.'

Hearing his name being bandied about, Pommes Frites stood up and wagged his tail.

'Yes, yes, Pamplemousse,' said Monsieur Leclercq wearily. 'I do recall the escapade, although I must admit it happened so long ago the precise details escape me. When I said "poor woman" I was referring to Madame Chavignol, not the inflatable nun.'

'I read recently of a carrier that has been developed in order to move transformers on cushions of air between the factory and the power station,' continued Monsieur Pamplemousse, unwilling to be deflected from his theme. 'Some of them can support as much as 300 tonnes.'

'I hardly think Madame Chavignol makes a habit of sharing her bed with a three hundred tonne transformer,' said the Director impatiently. 'At the time I felt she was in need of counselling, not electric shock treatment. I have since learnt better.'

Monsieur Pamplemousse raised his eyebrows and waited patiently while the Director toyed nervously with a propelling pencil.

'I have an idea I would like to run up the flagpole, Aristide,' he said at long last. 'But it must not go beyond these four walls.'

'You have been to *les Etats-Unis* recently, *Monsieur*?' It was a long established fact that whenever the Director visited America he invariably returned armed with the latest jargon, although by the time he started dropping it into the conversation more often than not it was long past its sell-by date.

'I have only just returned, as matter of fact. I had to address a seminar at the CIA...'

'You have been to the Pentagon, *Monsieur*?' In spite of everything Monsieur Pamplemousse couldn't help being impressed. 'I didn't know their canteen had been awarded an honorary Stock Pot. If I may offer my congratulations, that is a splendid gesture. It can do nothing but good. Franco-American relations often seem at a low ebb. Only last night Mademoiselle Odette was complaining about the recent flood of hamburger bars in the Champs Elysées.'

'No, Pamplemousse,' the Director broke in impatiently. 'You misunderstand me. I am not referring to the Central Intelligence Agency, but to the Culinary Institute of America. Both, I may say, have equally high standards, even if they differ somewhat in their ideals. The main difference between the two is that whereas the Intelligence Agency are much like our own Direction Général de la Sécurité – they cannot resist placing bugs wherever they go, – the latter spend their time making sure none exist. Food poisoning is ever uppermost in their minds. Cleanliness is certainly next to Godliness with those who attend classes at the school's premises in New York State.

Certificates are not awarded lightly.

'However, that is not why I wished to see you. I have other matters to discuss. Matters of extreme delicacy.'

Once again, Monsieur Leclercq cast a nervous eye towards his office door. 'What I am about to tell you, Aristide, must be treated in the utmost confidence.

'That very same evening, when I found myself one of a party of twelve at dinner, I had a strange experience. In the beginning Chavignol was at one end of the table, his wife at the other.

'Early in the meal the discussion became rather heated on the subject of Fusion cooking. It began with the first course, which was *grenouilles* in *wonton* soup. I had no quarrel with the freshness of the frog's legs. As one of the other guests, an Englishman, remarked – they were so fresh they were practically doing the breast stroke.'

'*Les Anglais* have a bizarre sense of humour, *Monsieur*. They find it hard to take anything seriously. One has to admire them.'

Monsieur Leclerq brushed the interruption to one side. 'Nor could I find fault with the cooking. It was simply that it was a clash of cultures and against many of the principles we hold dear in *Le Guide*. It was not for nothing that our Founder decided to use the symbol of a Stock Pot rather than a wok as a sign of excellence.

'Much as I admired the skill which went into the dish, it is at such times that I fear for the future of France. Why do we award Stock Pots, if not for the appreciation of French food? If I say the words *boudin noir*, Aristide, what name springs to mind?'

'Dijon, *Monsieur*. It is near there that the annual sausage festival takes place.'

'Exactly. Our own symbol, the humble *escargot*, evokes a similar response. Mention it and one immediately thinks of Martigny and their annual snail Festival.'

'Where else, *Monsieur*?'

'By the same token, I shudder to think what the members of the *Confrérie des Taste Cuisses de Grenouilles de Vittel* would have to say about a dish which consisted of frogs legs in Chinese soup. I'm afraid I became rather heated on the subject.

'However, things calmed down and by the time we reached the fromage stage, it was suggested – I think by Madame Chavignol herself – that we should all change places in order to get to know each other better. Little did I guess what was in her mind!

'Soon after we resumed eating I was talking to a lady on my right who worked for the Banque de France – we were discussing the state of the economy, about which, I have to say, she seemed remarkably ignorant – when I felt something crawling up the inside of my right leg. I daresay you have heard of people playing what is known in some circles as *faire du pied*?'

'It is a game for two, played beneath the table, *Monsieur*. I believe the English call it footsie.'

'That doesn't surprise me. It is yet another side to *les Anglais*. They equate everything in terms of sport. But this was something else again. Whatever it was, it moved in snake-like fashion, slowly and inexorably up the inside of my leg until it could go no further. It was only then, when it began to wiggle, that I realised it was a toe. I will leave you to guess the sex.'

'Was it a digit of the female persuasion, *Monsieur*?'

'It was, and it needed very little persuading.'

'The big one?'

'The size is immaterial, Pamplemousse. Although I have to admit that by then whoever it belonged to must have realised it hadn't had as far to travel as she might have anticipated, and the distance was getting less with every passing moment. I hesitate to say it had been met halfway, but it had, metaphorically speaking, hit the buffers.'

Monsieur Leclercq paused for a moment to mop his brow. There was the sound of lapping water as Pommes Frites, who had been hanging on the Director's every word and gesture, made the most of the opportunity.

Monsieur Pamplemousse looked at his boss. It must be costing him dearly to bare his soul in this way.

'I know what you are thinking, Aristide,' said Monsieur Leclercq. 'You are thinking if this ever gets out the reputation of *Le Guide* will plummet.'

It was, in fact, the last thing on Monsieur Pamplemousse's mind, but he could see why the Director might be worried. A scandal could have severe repercussions in financial circles.

'By then I had quite lost the thread of the conversation with the lady from the bank. I must have been sweating like a pig, for I remember her asking me if I was feeling unwell.

'I looked around the table and by process of elimination decided that even though Madame Chavignol was engaged in animated conversation with her neighbours on either side, the foot could only belong to her. No one else at the table had legs that long and even she must have been stretching hers to their fullest extent.

'Shortly afterwards, a second *pied* began to make its presence felt. Having established a foothold as it were, it set about manoeuvring my left leg into a complimentary position on her side of the table. And there it stayed, locked in a vicelike grip between her thighs for the rest of the meal.

'When we eventually rose there was a thud and I realised my shoe had become detached. Fortunately I had the presence of mind to discard its companion, otherwise my limp might have given the game away.

'Worse was to follow. My wife was taking a stroll in the garden with one of the other guests, and I had just asked Madame Chavignol if she had read any good books lately – one has to keep up the charade in these situations, when she took me by the arm and led me towards some kind of outbuilding clearly reserved for the laundering of garments – there was a distinct odour of disinfectant in the air; it quite negated the smell of the scented candles outside. As we entered I detected the sound of machinery. She appeared to be nervous. On the way there she kept looking at her watch.

'When I complained that the smell was giving me a headache she produced a tablet from a gold locket she wore round her neck. She said it would do me the world of good.'

'Do you know what it was?' asked Monsieur Pamplemousse.

'It had a strange name. Rather like that famous American waterfall – Niagara...'

Monsieur Pamplemousse stared at the Director. For all his worldliness, he had moments of quite breathtaking naivety.

'And you took it, *Monsieur*?'

'Of course. I could hardly refuse. In fact, she gave me three. I must confess I sensed a certain amount of impatience on her part. They proved most efficacious. Almost immediately I began to feel better.

'It was at that point that she suddenly began uttering cries of '*Vite! Vite!*' Seating herself on one of the machines, she kicked a box into place by my feet and drew me towards her. I felt her legs encircle my body. Strictly between ourselves, Aristide, I can hardly claim it was an unpleasant sensation. It was also considerably enhanced by the soft vibration of the machine itself. But that was as far as it went until suddenly, almost as though it had taken on a life of its own and had become imbued with the spirit of the occasion, the motor sprang into life. The speed increased some tenfold. It was like being in a ship at sea in a severe gale.'

Monsieur Pamplemousse gave a whistle. 'It sounds as though it could have gone into the spin-drying mode, *Monsieur*. At such times washing machines can reach a speed of anything up to two thousand revs a minute. They sound like an aeroplane about to take off.'

Privately he couldn't help but admire Madame Chavignol's split second timing. It was no wonder she had kept on looking at her watch.

'By that time two revs would have been more than sufficient,' said the Director feelingly. 'I had to hold on to Madame Chavignol for dear life! Just at the *moment critique* there was a blinding flash. At first I thought the machine had given up under the strain, then I realised it was someone with a camera. It was *coitus interruptus* with a vengeance!'

'These things happen, *Monsieur*.'

'They may well happen to you, Pamplemousse, but I have certainly never experienced anything like it either before or since. I tell you, it is one thing talking about it in the cold light of day, but it was quite another matter on a sultry autumn evening in the 7th *arrondissement*.

'It is an old saying but a true one, Aristide, "Never choose your women or your linen by candlelight".

'However, that is not the worst of the story. A few days later I received a bombshell in the mail. There was no note, just a photograph. Fortunately Chantal didn't open it, for I need hardly tell you what it depicted.

'My initial reaction was that it was a kind thought on the part of Madame Chavignol, but when I visited her and asked for the return of the negative she was a different person to the one who had unburdened herself to me only a few days before.

'Do you know what she said?'

Monsieur Pamplemousse shook his head, although he had a shrewd idea.

'"You men are all the same. You and all the others." She even had the gall to laugh in my face and point towards the stairs. From all she said, I strongly suspect my picture is not the only one she has there. My guess would be that she keeps them in her boudoir. Doubtless in a safe.'

'*Alors!*'

The Director shuddered. '*Alors!* is right, Aristide.'

'You mentioned earlier about running an idea up the flagpole,' said Monsieur Pamplemousse, breaking the long silence. 'If there is anything I can do...'

Monsieur Leclercq's face cleared. As if by magic the lines disappeared from his face as he rose and circumnavigated the desk.

'I knew I could rely on you, Aristide!' he exclaimed. 'You have never let me down yet.'

That hadn't been quite what Monsieur Pamplemousse meant. He had a distinct feeling of impending doom.

'I want the negative back,' continued the Director. 'And I want it back along with any other prints before the police get there.

'Inevitably, given the circumstances, they will be going through Chavignol's past life looking for clues as to who might be responsible for his murder. They will leave no stone unturned. Papers will be inspected, letters perused, photographs unearthed, fingers will be pointed...

'You, of all people, Pamplemousse, should know that.'

'I understand what you are saying, *Monsieur*. But I don't see how I can possibly help.'

'It is perfectly simple, Aristide. All you need do is find the person responsible for the demise of Monsieur Chavignol and the police will consider the matter closed. Then you will be able to break into the safe at your leisure.'

It was Monsieur Pamplemousse's turn to clutch at straws. 'Unfortunately,' he said, 'my services are already bespoke. I have received an offer from a well-known *journal*.'

'No man can serve two masters, Aristide,' said Monsieur Leclercq severely. 'It is written in the scriptures: Matthew 6:24.'

That answered the question. Monsieur Pamplemousse felt tempted to suggest that at the time of his writing the scriptures, probably laboriously carving them in stone, Matthew wasn't working for *Le Guide*, nor in all probability had he ever met anyone quite like the Director, but clearly the subject was not up for discussion.

Monsieur Leclercq rose to his feet. 'I was thinking on the way in,' he continued, 'the whole sorry affair must have been a shock for Pommes Frites too... seeing you on the screen like that. Your wife was telling me all about it. It appears he thought you were trapped somewhere inside the receiver. I suggest you need to spend some quality time with him and I can think of no better way of making a start than the two of you taking a quiet stroll and offering your condolences to Madame Chavignol. At the same time you can familiarise yourself with the premises, perhaps picking up a few clues while you are there.'

Seeing the look on Monsieur Pamplemousse's face, the Director clasped his shoulder.

'It seems to me,' he said, 'that given the presence of the

boxes in the laundry room, and the expert way in which Madame Chavignol manoeuvred the appropriate one into position, she'd had plenty of practice at estimating her victim's measurements over the years. The contents of her safe, if that is indeed where the photographs are kept, could rock the establishment to its very foundations.

'I know this is supposed to be your week off, Aristide, but remember this: you are not doing it simply as a favour to me, you will also be doing it for France. It will not go unnoticed I can assure you.'

Short of joining Monsieur Leclercq in singing the national anthem, there was really nothing more to be said.

'I would come with you, Aristide, but...'

But you can't face seeing her again in the cold light of day, thought Monsieur Pamplemousse.

'...I have another commitment,' continued the Director, as though reading his thoughts. 'Duty calls, I am afraid.'

On the way out of the building Monsieur Pamplemousse met Véronique coming in. She had with her a carrier bag imprinted with the insignia of a well-known fashion designer.

'Cheer up,' she said. 'And take care. I wouldn't like you to end up in Madame Chavignol's safe along with all the others.'

Truly a man had no secrets from his secretary, even if there were times when he did have to pay dearly for the privilege. There was a price for everything in this world.

Chapter Four

It was past midday before Monsieur Pamplemousse found the address the Director had given him.

Within sight of the top of the Eiffel Tower and yet to all intents and purposes a million miles away, it was typical of that part of Paris where ministries, museums and foreign embassies proliferate to such an extent that a casual passer by might be forgiven for thinking noone actually lived there.

Yet that was far from being the case. Behind forbidding entrances all over the 7th there lay a closed world of ancient homes, former mansions, eighteenth century *hôtels*, and secret gardens; a throwback to the days of Napoleon, who had preserved the area partly in celebration of his military victories, but also with an eye to feathering his own nest by creating a new nobility under the guise of preserving continuity. Books galore had been written about them, but unless you happened to strike lucky and be passing by when their doors were open to allow passage in or out, or had the kind of wealth that opened them for you, few revealed themselves to strangers.

He was about to make use of a heraldic knocker on a pair of heavy oak doors in a wall not far from the Basilique Sainte-Clotilde, when he noticed a discreet video entry-phone let into the stonework to one side. Pressing a button elicited an almost immediate response.

After a slight pause while whoever was at the other end digested his name and business, no doubt at the same time studying the card he held up to the lens (he purposely made sure his thumb covered any mention of *Le Guide*), a voice asked him to wait. Some half a minute or so passed before a buzzer sounded. It was followed by a muffled click from behind the nearest of the two doors.

Signalling Pommes Frites to follow, Monsieur Pamplemousse pushed open a smaller inset door and went in. He almost expected to be greeted by a footman in full livery. Instead, as the door automatically closed behind them, another opened on the far side of a cobbled courtyard and a very small Asian in a white jacket emerged, beckoning them forward. He looked like the actor Peter Lorre in an early Mr. Moto film.

Casting his eyes around as he went, Monsieur Pamplemousse glanced up at the building. It was more like a country mansion than a town house: a well protected one at that! High up on the walls, strategically placed CCTV cameras covered the area he was in, leaving him feeling naked and vulnerable. The upper windows were protected by white shutters, whilst those on the ground floor had stout metal grills.

To the left of the house there was a stable-block garage. The row of steel up-and-over doors was shut, as was another door, presumably a tradesman's entrance, in a wall between the two buildings. The Facel Vega he had seen standing outside the studios the night before was parked alongside it. Someone must have moved fast. Perhaps they needed the space.

In passing he seized the opportunity to take a closer look. Only one hundred and fifty-two had been built in the three years before the company went into liquidation and since most of them went for export he might never see another. Comparing it to his own *Deux Chevaux* was like comparing chalk and cheese. Nearly four million of the latter had been made.

The Excellence had an American Chrysler V8 6.3 litre engine, and with its armchair type front seat it was nothing short of decadence on wheels; for most of its life, the 2CV – a deckchair on wheels as some people called it – had been propelled by a simple 375cc engine. The one thing they had in common was that they were both products of the drawing board and both were idiosyncratic. At least his car was easy to climb in and out of; the Excellence with its pillarless construction might be sexy, but its doors had acquired an unhappy reputation for occasionally staying firmly shut when you wanted to get out.

As he neared the main entrance to the house he noted the front door was as solid as those at the main gate. There would be no breaking through its panels in a hurry. Removing his coat before entering he had a fleeting glimpse of welded security pins on the inward opening hinges.

One way and another, he knew all he wished to know for the time being. The 7th had a reputation for being the most closely guarded *arrondissement* in Paris; there were gendarmes everywhere. Jules Romain had hit the nail on the head when he called it "a capital within a capital". To add so much security on top of what already existed seemed an unnecessary gilding of the lily; a belt and braces operation, but no doubt the Chavignols had their reasons.

While the Japanese manservant relieved him of his coat, executing a series of bows as he backed away, a woman he took to be Madame Chavignol appeared further down the hall. Glancing briefly at a small pile of unopened letters on a table as she passed, she came forward to greet him, hand outstretched.

'Monsieur Pamplemousse. It is kind of you to come. I hadn't expected...'

71

'It was the least I could do.'

'But so soon...'

Her hand felt cold rather than cool. She held on to his for a fraction of a second longer than seemed necessary while she scrutinised him. Then, letting go, she turned and motioned him to follow. He couldn't help thinking that apart from dark glasses there was no question of her being in deep mourning.

Nor was the flow of inconsequential chatter she kept up what he would have expected from a person in a state of shock. Or, perhaps it was. Perhaps he was doing her an injustice and it was some kind of defence mechanism at work.

All the same, after the Director's graphic revelations he was prepared for almost anything.

From the length of her elegantly cut dark hair, he guessed she must be still in her early thirties. She was wearing a white shirt and black trousers – with very little, if anything, underneath either if he was any judge in the matter. The rest was a model of expensive understatement: Hermès belt, black suede mules; silver earrings, each with a single diamond set in the middle; she was coolness personified. A white gold brooch and a white gold Cartier wrist watch completed the ensemble.

Although black predominated, it wasn't exactly widow's weeds.

He caught a whiff of perfume. Expensively discreet would have been a fair description. And yet, he couldn't help being aware of something else over-riding it; something much more mundane and very familiar. So familiar he couldn't immediately put a name to it. Sandalwood? No – simpler than that. Almonds? He had almonds on the brain.

Pommes Frites obviously noticed it too. Although, having registered it, he kept his thoughts to himself for the time being.

Nor could it be said that her late husband was into counting his Euros. As she led the way towards the rear of the house by way of an enormous lounge, he took stock of his surroundings. At some time the room they were passing through had been stripped, a purist might say vandalised, of what must once have been all the trappings of an ornately furnished salon. The walls had the kind of sheen that only came from many applications of paint. The floor had been re-laid with hardwood, polished until you could see your face in it.

Only the ceiling decorations had been left intact.

Apart from the fact that there seemed to be two of everything, it reminded him of a Philippe Starck exhibition he and Doucette had once been to see.

There were two enormous sofas – each large enough to seat a whole family; two mammoth plasma screen television sets; two chandeliers; two harps! What would anyone want with two harps? Madame Chavignol didn't look the sort of person who would spend the long winter evenings perfecting her *arpeggios*.

There were flowers everywhere: freshly cut lilies and iris in enormous vases; the kind of displays you normally only came across in three Stock Pot restaurants, or on yachts in the south of France during the season. A Hermès Birkin handbag left carelessly open on a table was something more than a fashion statement.

Abstract paintings dotted the walls. A brief glance was enough. He knew what he liked, and on the whole it didn't extend to large pieces of canvas that looked as though a child had ridden across them on its tricycle, having first passed through several trays of primary coloured paint. Many of them were unframed, although they had proba-

73

bly cost the earth.

On a corner table just inside the door there was a sprinkling of statuettes and silver cups, and on the wall behind it a number of framed certificates. Presumably they all belonged to Monsieur Chavignol; show biz mementos. Somehow they summed everything up.

It was all too perfect and unlived in, with not a sign of a book anywhere; sad in its way, as though the house and its contents had been left in the hands of a designer and the table was the only concession he had allowed the owner for his personal effects.

Bringing up the rear and clearly feeling in need of a rest after their long walk, Pommes Frites paused by a thick pile rug and eyed it hopefully.

Catching sight of him out of the corner of her eye, Madame Chavignol broke off for a moment. 'Your dog looks thirsty. Does he prefer still or sparkling water?'

'Given the choice, he prefers still.'

'I will have Yin him bring some Evian.'

Motioning Pommes Frites to remain where he was, Monsieur Pamplemousse followed her out onto a patio which at first sight was as immaculately tidy as the inside of the house. Concealed lamps dotted around the perimeter no doubt doubled as either heat, or movement-sensitive security lights by night. Through thick glass portholes let into the paving he could see an underground swimming pool, bathed in blue light.

The scene beyond them was like a stage set, probably the work of the same interior designer. There was hardly a leaf out of place. The elegance of it all made his own herb collection seem very small fry, but at least his was a hands-on operation.

He began to wish he had worn another suit, but then Monsieur Leclercq hadn't given him the opportunity to go home and change.

'How strange that my husband should die in your arms,' said Madame Chavignol. 'It must have been a shock to you.'

'You saw it happen?' asked Monsieur Pamplemousse.

She nodded. 'Normally I would have been in the studio, but last night I chose to stay at home and watched it all on television instead. I don't know if that made it worse – my not being there – but even if I had been I couldn't have done anything. It was all over so quickly. It's just... I know I shall always regret not being with him at the end.'

Seating herself in a white painted lounge seat with matching cushions, she motioned him towards a more formal upright chair facing her. Between the two of them, but slightly to one side, there was a slatted garden table.

As Monsieur Pamplemousse made himself comfortable he noticed two champagne glasses, one of which was still half full.

'Forgive me. Have I called at an inconvenient moment?'

'Not at all.' She brushed his protest to one side. 'It was all so sudden... the staff are shattered, of course. But they are carrying on as normal. Claude... my husband and I always tried to have lunch together. It was part of our routine.'

Reaching down, she picked up a telephone, put through the order for Pommes Frites' water, then paused. 'In fact...' she looked at her watch, 'since it is almost twelve-thirty, perhaps you will do me the honour of joining me?'

It wasn't what he had bargained on, but obviously it hadn't occurred to her that he might refuse. It wasn't so much an invitation as a command.

'I imagine the police have been in touch with you,' said Monsieur Pamplemousse, as she replaced the receiver.

'They were here last night and again this morning. They

are awaiting the report of the autopsy. Until that is done I can't begin to make arrangements with a funeral director. But there seems little doubt as to the cause. They say it was cyanide.'

Monsieur Pamplemousse wondered whether he should mention the offending oyster shell, but decided to play it by ear.

'And you have no idea how it came about – or who might have been responsible?'

Madame Chavignol shook her head. 'None. Claude had his enemies, of course. Who doesn't? That is especially true if you happen to be in the public eye. But as for deliberately poisoning him...'

She waited a moment or two while the manservant appeared, filled both the glasses from a bottle of Louis Roederer Cristal and began setting the table for two; stainless steel place mats – again in the shape of an interlocking double C – Christofle cutlery, Riedel glasses.

Monsieur Pamplemousse took the opportunity to take a closer look at the garden. Beyond the patio, sunlight filtered through the trees, illuminating a mixture of styles: freshly raked gravel paths, their curves contrasting with the straight lines of others made of old stone paving; little nooks and crannies housing unrestrained shrubs surrounded by clipped box hedging; old shrub roses and clematis planted alongside more formal beds.

Barely audible soft music came from hidden loudspeakers. Fish played in a pool watched over by a pair of bronze herons. Other pieces of sculpture were dotted around; a rotunda here, a domed arbour made of distressed pinewood there.

The whole was surrounded by ancient ivy-covered stone walls, recessed in places for ornaments. From where he was sitting it was hard to tell what lay immediately behind them.

One thing was certain. The Director had a problem on his hands if he was hoping to get his negatives back by devious means. The place was like a fortress.

'I still think it is an extraordinary coincidence that you should be at the studio yesterday evening,' said Madame Chavignol when they were alone again. 'Do you often go?'

'It was my first visit.'

'Well, then...'

'Perhaps it was meant,' said Monsieur Pamplemousse simply.

Catching her looking at him he elaborated. 'Who is to say what is a coincidence and what is preordained?'

'Who indeed?' said Madame Chavignol thoughtfully.

At least she seemed to have no idea of his connection with *Le Guide*. There was no reason why she should of course, but it made his task easier. Having said that, the plain truth was he had no idea where to lead the conversation. It was all very well for the Director, sending him off to spy out the territory. But having established a bridgehead as it were, what next?

He was acutely aware of her surveying him across the top of her champagne glass. Her long legs were crossed, the upper one moving slowly up and down like a metronome. It was a well-known syndrome – he had come across it before. As ever he couldn't help being reminded of the offshore oil derricks common to the West Coast of California; inexorable, regular, hypnotic, like the pecking ducks that had been all the rage in souvenir shops at one time.

Under different circumstances he might have suspected her of doing it on purpose, but it didn't feel that way. It was hard to tell what was going on behind those dark glasses. If anything she seemed preoccupied with her own thoughts, just as he was with his.

It was hard to picture her sitting on top of a washing machine; those same elegant legs encircling Monsieur Leclercq, drawing him ever closer towards her; the Director holding on like grim death as the motor gathered speed. But then that was often the case with other people's peccadilloes. The older he got the more he found nothing surprised him any more.

'What are you thinking?'

Monsieur Pamplemousse came to his senses with a start. She would probably be mortified if he told her the truth. Concentrate Pamplemousse!

'May I call you Aristide?' she continued. 'I can't keep calling you by your surname. Besides, you don't look at all like a grapefruit.' Her voice was soft and low. Perhaps she was musical after all.

'Please do.'

'Your name was in all the *journaux* this morning,' she said, by way of explanation. 'And your photograph. They all seemed to think it was something of a coincidence too. I gather you were very famous during your time with the *Sûreté*. One of them likened you to a dog with a bone. You never gave up.'

'The media always fasten on these things,' said Monsieur Pamplemousse. 'It gives an added edge to their stories. You shouldn't pay too much attention to them...' He didn't know whether to call her Madame or use her full title.

She solved the problem for him. 'Please call me Claudette. It was a little joke Claude and I had. He always called me his "little Claudette".'

When she smiled her teeth were flawless. Small, regular and flawless, they lit up her face. He wondered how many people she had dug them into over the years. The Director clearly wasn't the only one by a long chalk.

'I call my wife "Couscous",' said Monsieur Pamplemousse. 'When we first met I took her out to dinner one evening. It was on the fringes of the 18th and all we could find were middle eastern restaurants. It became a joke and somehow it stuck.'

'There you are,' said Claudette. 'Talking of bones...' She picked up the phone again and issued an order.

Monsieur Pamplemousse felt himself warming to her.

She replaced the receiver. 'May I ask you something?'

'Of course...'

'Everything happened so suddenly; I don't know which way to turn. It isn't that I don't trust the police, but... I have never before felt so alone...'

He had an inkling of what she was going to say, but it all came out in a rush.

It never rained but what it poured. It was the third time he'd been asked to take on the case in as many hours. It seemed to him that everyone wanted to use him for their own ends.

In the case of the *journal* it was a straightforward business proposition; a desire to steal a march over their rivals along with the added bonus of all the publicity that would go with it. With Monsieur Leclercq it had been the reverse; fear of publicity was undoubtedly at the bottom of it; fear of the effect it would have on *Le Guide* and on his personal reputation should the photographs be revealed, not to mention the fact that his life at home wouldn't be worth living.

Madame Chantal Leclercq had a reputation for keeping her husband on a very short lead. There had been the occasion when he had indulged in a brief dalliance with an English *au pair* called Elsie. She had soon put a stop to that!

And now came the third offer. It was understandable

that Claudette should want to get to the bottom of her husband's murder, but it was early days. Perhaps she was simply clutching at straws.

He was saved giving an immediate answer by the arrival of the first course: chicken *consommé*, to which some well ripened chopped tomatoes had been added at the time of clarifying. The skins must have been left on, for it was a delicate pink colour. Served cold in a cup, it was deliciously refreshing; fully worthy of a Stock Pot in *Le Guide*.

'Superb!' Monsieur Pamplemousse signified his approval as he dabbed at his lips with the napkin.

'*Merci*. Yang is an absolute marvel. He came at the same time as Yin. I call them Yin and Yang because that is the way they are. Yin, as you have seen, is dark and can be very negative at times. Yang, the chef, is bright and positive. He helps... *helped* my husband with his recipes for the programme.'

Created them more like it, if this soup is anything to go by, thought Monsieur Pamplemousse. There was a confidence about the dish that showed a master hand at work.

Along with more champagne, a bottle of Chateldon water appeared.

'And yesterday's dish – the single oyster – that was Yang's idea?'

'No, that was entirely Claude's doing. Normally the routine was that we would have lunch together and he would go to the studios later in the day. All the technical rehearsals and run-throughs took place with a stand-in during the morning and early afternoon. He was brought up in the tradition of the stage and he liked to keep things as fresh as possible. That was another reason for having an audience – he was at his best with a spontaneous reaction.'

The first course was followed by lobster salad; the lobster cut into small pieces and mixed in with equal portions of diced cucumber and brown rice.

The cucumber was crisp, having been well salted and drained. Seasoned with an olive oil and vinegar dressing, it had been lightly peppered and sprinkled with finely chopped chervil. The brown Italian rice had been cooked in chicken stock and seasoned with grated nutmeg. The whole had been garnished with a sprinkling of chopped black olives.

A white Meursault accompanied the dish. He tried to catch the label, but it was covered by a napkin. He guessed at a Lafon. Unrefined, yet splendidly elegant.

'Is the wine your chef's choice too?'

Claudette nodded. 'I shall be sorry to lose him,' she said wryly.

'Will that be necessary?'

'I doubt if he will want to stay on just for me. Who knows? He may wish to open his own restaurant. I know someone who may be able to help him.'

I bet you do, thought Monsieur Pamplemousse. 'How long has he been with you?'

'Long enough for me to know him as well as I know the next person.'

'Did he have anything to do with the preparation of the oyster?'

'He wouldn't do such a thing if that's what you are thinking. I would trust him with my life.'

And you, thought Monsieur Pamplemousse again, must be a Leo to be so sure of yourself.

'What happened yesterday afternoon? You followed the same routine?'

'Yesterday there was even less to do. Claude didn't go in until much later than usual. As I say, he only had the single oyster to take with him. The seaweed was provided by

81

the studio.'

A sudden breeze funnelling through neighbouring buildings caused a slight downdraft and as the leaves began to rustle he saw what looked like a minotaur peering at him from behind a colonnade. A bird pecking at a piece of bread took flight, carrying what was left in its beak.

Claudette gave a shiver. 'At least it meant we had more time together. Perhaps you are right when you say some things are meant. I cannot believe it was simply a coincidence, any more than your being here today is. That is why I feel I need your help. You are so much more thorough than the police. They hardly asked any questions.'

Monsieur Pamplemousse shrugged. 'Everyone has their methods. I am a Capricorn. Capricorns may take their time, but they get there in the end.'

The meat course was *compote* of baby rabbit in vegetable aspic, along with mushroom, button onions, tiny carrots and herbs – he detected tarragon, chervil and chives.

The *gelée* itself had been well clarified; clear and sparkling, it kept its shape without being at all rubbery.

With it came red Bordeaux. A Château Pichon-Longeville Baron '90. He wondered if Claudette always lunched as well, or whether she was putting on a special display for his benefit. Obviously it must be the former since he had arrived unannounced. The loss of her husband certainly hadn't affected her appetite.

He was longing to get at the notebook he kept concealed in the right leg of his trousers for just such occasions. The whole thing was such an unexpected bonus. If Yang did open a restaurant it could be a welcome addition to *Le Guide*; a feather in his own cap for being first with the news.

'May I offer you a cup of drinking chocolate?'

Once again she seemed to be reading his thoughts. 'I follow the Montignac method of keeping fit. Three good meals a day, with nothing in between. Don't totally give up what you really crave for, but enjoy it in moderation. Chocolate being his particular weakness, he manages to include it in his regime. He maintains it is good for the digestion. Provided it is over 70% pure cocoa, of course.'

'Of course,' said Monsieur Pamplemousse drily, then went on: 'But cooking can also be an art; a matter of inspiration, a performance. It is like acting. In a world that is populated by countless millions of people, some actors have only to utter a few words and you know at once who it is.

'Chefs speak with their food. Their world has an infinite variety of ingredients, but there are the select few who are able to combine them in such a way that their voice is immediately recognisable. That is where actors have the advantage. Their voices can be recorded; great meals are things of the moment; created only to be consumed.

'I am not surprised your chef is Japanese. Up to now it has been more a case of French chefs spending time in the Orient. Fusion cookery is now the current buzzword. There is no reason why there shouldn't be a movement in the opposite direction: Japanese chefs coming over here and taking us on at what we believe to be our home ground.'

'You seem very knowledgeable on the subject.'

Monsieur Pamplemousse realised he had better soft-pedal his connection with food. Not for the first time his enthusiasm was getting the better of him. A few minutes earlier he had been racking his brains trying to think of a way of turning the conversation to suit his own purposes, now he had taken it up another blind alley.

Claudette did it for him. Raising her sunglasses until

they rested on top of her head, she leaned forward, gently touched his knee and gazed into his eyes.

'I shall miss Claude's voice.'

Her eyes were green. Arguably the deepest green he had ever seen. He wondered if she wore coloured contact lenses. If that were the case, combined with the unusually dark glasses it was a wonder she found her way around at all.

'You don't have to answer now. But... please think it over. Let me have your card, then at least I shall have someone to call on if I need help...'

'I'm sorry, I don't carry one.' Monsieur Pamplemousse had a mental picture of Doucette answering the phone and his reply was automatic. All too late he remembered he had produced his card at the gate, but Claudette appeared not to notice.

For a moment he thought she was about to cry. Then, as swiftly as she had moved towards him she withdrew her hand from his knee.

There was a crash as the bottle of wine went flying.

'*Mon Dieu!*' Grabbing hold of the napkin he began dabbing at his trousers, but it was already too late; he could feel the liquid soaking into them. His first thought was for his precious notebook; his second for the Pichon-Longueville. His third, he had to admit, was for Madame Chavignol.

'Forgive me!'

'*Tant pis,*' said Monsieur Pamplemousse. 'Never mind.'

'But I do mind!'

So vivid had been Monsieur Leclercq's description of his indiscretions, the possibility flashed through Monsieur Pamplemousse's mind that the whole thing might be a ploy with a visit to the laundry-room in mind. He immediately rejected the thought as without the slightest hesitation she picked up the phone and called for help.

Within seconds Yin came running armed with a fresh roll of paper towel.

'Please to come with me,' he said interpreting his mistress's hurried instructions.

'Take your time!' Claudette set about clearing away the pieces of broken glass. She seemed genuinely mortified.

Transported upstairs in double quick time and finding himself in what appeared to be the master bedroom, Monsieur Pamplemousse was quick to take advantage of the situation. It was an ill wind that blew nobody any good.

Having been shown the *en-suite* bathroom, he dismissed Yin and as soon as he heard the door close behind him, removed his shoes, socks and trousers and set off on a quick tour of the bedroom.

Two king size beds dominated the room. A brief inspection of a cupboard with sliding doors running the length of one wall failed to reveal any nuns, with or without their habits. There were certainly no transformers! So much for Claudette's tale of woe regarding her marital problems!

He turned his attention to the wall behind the beds. Between the two there was a cabinet, the top of which acted as a shelf for bedside lights, and inside, behind glass doors, there was a row of identical books, bound in tooled leather and all in pristine condition, rather as though they had been bought by the yard to decorate a film set. They looked as though they had never been opened, and perhaps never would be.

Higher up the wall hung a large painting. It was in a completely different style to any of those he'd seen downstairs.

Oil on canvas, it was signed by an artist called John Bratby. Even though the subject's forehead had been rendered a deep purple, it was clearly an impression of

Claude Chavignol – the more so the further away you were. Perhaps he had been in a bad mood at the time, for there was something funny about the eyes. Not only were they looking in different directions, but they didn't seem to be following him around the room as eyes in portrait paintings normally did.

It was that more than anything that led him to feel behind the canvas. His fingers encountered a large metal plate. He didn't try moving it in case it was magnetic, set to trigger an alarm should anyone try to remove it before it was disarmed. He guessed the safe behind it must have a coded combination lock. There wasn't room for anything else.

Quickly returning to the bathroom in case anyone came in, Monsieur Pamplemousse examined his trousers. Hastily removing his precious notebook before the liquid penetrated its pages, he placed it on top of a radiator for safekeeping.

Looking around the room and seeing his reflection multiplied a hundred fold in the mirrored walls and ceiling, it was hard to escape the uncanny feeling that the world was somehow closing in on him. Perhaps it was yet another manifestation of Monsieur Chavignol's tastes.

Undoing his shirt cuffs, he looked around to see where to turn on the basin tap, only to discover it came on automatically when he put his hands under the outlet. The sink plug sank gently into place as soon the water reached the correct temperature.

At the same time stereophonic strains of *The Blue Danube* issued from concealed loudspeakers.

Standing over the basin sponging his trousers with cold water, lulled into a state of euphoria by the music, Monsieur Pamplemousse felt his heart going out to Claudette.

He still hadn't got the measure of her. It wasn't that he disbelieved the Director's story – he could hardly have dreamt the whole thing – but her remorse at having spilt the wine over him had been palpable, *and* she had unhesitatingly taken immediate action. There had been no question of allowing him to brush it aside.

Underneath it all she could be a woman in need of help; vulnerable and alone. Possibly when she went to bed at night and looked at herself in the mirror she was like millions of others the world over, wishing things were different. Women always did. All the ones he had known, anyway. Doucette worried about her nose. Others dreamed of being taller, shorter, thinner, fatter, bigger breasted, smaller breasted; anything but what they were. Magazines devoted their pages to such problems.

It was hard to picture what Claudette might want to change. Not knowing might even be a worry in itself. Sometimes beauty had its drawbacks.

Hanging his trousers over a heated rail to dry, he hesitated for a moment, wondering whether to take advantage of a pair of 'his' and 'hers' bathrobes hanging on the wall. Unable to make up his mind, he pushed the door open slightly to make sure the coast was clear, and found the room in darkness. Quite likely the light went off automatically if it was left unoccupied for any length of time. Given all the electronic gadgets there were around, it might even come on again as soon as he went back in.

Remembering the bedside lights, Monsieur Pamplemousse set off in what he hoped was the right direction.

He hadn't gone very far when he trod on something soft. Reaching down to disentangle whatever it was clinging to his toes, he froze as his hand met up with what felt remarkably like another foot, patently not his own.

Momentarily blinded by the sudden glare of a spotlight that came on somewhere in front of him, he jumped back as though he had been shot, and as his gaze travelled upwards it encountered a familiar head lying on a pillow of the bed to his right.

Wishing now that he hadn't left his trousers in the bathroom he instinctively made a grab for the nearest object.

Relieved of her bed cover, Claudette sat up, her arms outstretched invitingly.

Monsieur Pamplemousse backed away. All too clearly his suspicions as to what she may or may not have been wearing beneath her trousers when he first followed her through the house had been rendered academic.

Not that he had time to ponder the matter. The next moment she was on him; fighting, screaming, scratching like an unleashed tiger. And if her cries of *'Non, non, non,'* seemed singularly inappropriate under the circumstances, there was no time to dwell on that either. It felt as though he was engaged in a life and death struggle.

Busying himself on the floor below with the remains of the rabbit in aspic – some of the best he'd tasted in a long time – Pommes Frites pricked up his ears. He realised to his shame that he hadn't been concentrating quite as much as he might have done on what was going on around him.

True, he'd heard a crash, and then a few minutes after that he had seen his master go past accompanied by the man who had brought him his lunch. One or other of them had left a trail of drips behind. At first glance it had looked like blood, but a brief investigation established the fact that it was wine. Rather a good one in his opinion.

While he was savouring it a second figure had gone past, rather faster than the first two.

Something – it could have been a distant cry – told him his master was once again in trouble.

Following the smell of perfume, he tore out of the room and bounded up a flight of stairs two at a time.

Even when the scent came to an abrupt halt outside a door on the first floor he wasn't thrown. Grasping the handle between his teeth he turned it smartly in a clockwise direction until it would go no further, then gave a push with his right paw.

As it swung open his worst fears were confirmed. Bereft of his trousers, shirt hanging from one arm, Monsieur Pamplemousse looked in a sorry state.

It was no time for niceties. Without a moment's hesitation Pommes Frites hurled himself into the fray. The outcome as he landed, a paw on each shoulder of his master's assailant, was a foregone conclusion.

As the whole ensemble toppled over, ending up in a confused heap on the floor, he opened his mouth and prepared to deliver the *coup de grâce*.

The response, when it came, was eminently satisfactory: short, sharp and to the point; the accompanying shriek, more one of outrage than of pain, a compliment both to Pommes Frites' courage in the midst of danger and to his self-control when staring temptation in the face.

Chapter Five

'I shall have to stop going to the *laverie* in the Rue Caulaincourt!' said Doucette crossly. She held up a barely recognisable item of clothing. 'Just look at this shirt. Two minutes in the spin drier and there's not a single button left!'

Monsieur Pamplemousse avoided asking if there had been any buttons on it to start with. Remembering the state it had been in, he strongly suspected the answer would be no. The manner in which it had been torn from his body was not the kind of test normally favoured by consumer magazines.

'I should have complained at the time,' continued Doucette. 'Except those places are all the same. There's never anyone around when you need help. They're full of people gazing into space, waiting for something to happen. It's like entering a state of limbo.'

'Washing machines are responsible for a great many evils in this world,' said Monsieur Pamplemousse. 'If only they could talk, some of them would have a sorry tale to tell.'

Doucette ignored the remark. 'I can't understand it,' she persisted. 'It isn't as though the cotton needed renewing. I'm always careful to check it when I do the ironing.'

Searching in her bag, she produced another screwed-up ball of cloth. 'As for your trousers... they look as though they've been pulled through a hedge backwards with you inside them. I won't ask where you've been!'

Monsieur Pamplemousse offered up a silent prayer of thanks to his Guardian Angel, whoever it might be.

'That reminds me,' continued Doucette. 'Monsieur Leclercq was on the phone while you were out with Pommes Frites. He wants to see you. It sounded urgent as usual.'

'I expect he wants to talk about the *soufflé omelette* you made me two nights ago, Couscous,' said Monsieur Pamplemousse, trying to steer the conversation into calmer waters. 'I was telling him all about it – or trying to. It is hard to describe something which is really beyond description; the pleasure to be gained from the mathematical precision of the criss-cross lines imprinted by the poker on the *omelette*'s surface; the mouth-watering lightness of the inner texture; the taste of the rose-petal jam... I would hazard a guess that it was made from *Gloire de Dijon*. Everything about it was sheer perfection. I daresay Madame Leclercq would like the recipe.'

'I daresay pigs might fly,' said Doucette. 'I can't picture her slaving over a hot stove. Anyway, he sounded upset about something. He wants you in his office as soon as possible.'

Monsieur Pamplemousse sighed. 'It was supposed to be my week off.'

'The devil also finds work for idle hands,' said Doucette pointedly.

At least he looks after his own, thought Monsieur Pamplemousse, making good his escape before any more questions were asked. Once Doucette got the bit between her teeth there was no knowing where things would end up.

On the other hand, the same could be said of the Director. It was a wonder he hadn't been on the phone before. He must have arrived in his office rather later than usual for some reason. Perhaps his researches had taken him out of Paris.

Threading the *Deux Chevaux* through the tortuous maze of one-way streets leading down to the Place Clichy, he went over the previous day's events in his mind.

After making good his escape from the Chavignol residence, he had taken refuge in the tiny gardens of the Square Samuel-Rousseau, marshalling his thoughts as he dried out while Pommes Frites kept watch.

His encounter with Claudette had been a mind-boggling experience; one he wouldn't wish to repeat in a hurry. The Director had not been exaggerating. Once she got going she was like a woman possessed. There had been no stopping her. He told himself he should be thankful for small mercies; at least she didn't have a spin drier concealed in her *boudoir*.

The last of the summer flowers were still in bloom and with only an occasional solitary figure entering or leaving the Basilique Sainte Clotilde at the far end of the garden to disturb the peace, he had gradually come back down to earth again.

His recovery lasted all of thirty seconds. His heart missed a beat as a sudden thought struck him.

Wondering whether to try and reach Monsieur Leclercq on his mobile, he remembered the Director saying he had another appointment. It was a busy time in the office. Preparations for next year's guide were already getting into their stride and he was probably on his way to one or other of the eighteen restaurants in France singled out by the computer for the possible accolade of three Stock Pots.

'A hard job,' he was fond of saying, 'but someone has to do it.'

With most people it would have been meant as a joke, but in Monsieur Leclercq's case it was a serious statement of fact, and he had the waistline to prove it.

A quick call to Véronique confirmed his reading of the situation, and having persuaded her to put him through to the Director's personal voice mail, he had left a short message containing the single word *Estragon*. Known only to a select few, it was *Le Guide's* code word for an emergency, to be used only in extreme cases.

His second call had been to an ex-colleague from his days in the *Sûreté*. That, too, had been somewhat less than satisfactory. It wasn't that Jacques was unhelpful; non-committal was more the word. Clearly, for whatever reason, he hadn't wished to discuss the matter of Claude Chavignol's death over the phone.

Summing up, practically the only good thing to be said for the day was that at least Doucette was out when he arrived back home, and he had been able to change his clothes in peace. Now even that was in jeopardy. He wasn't out of the wood yet.

Some twenty minutes later, having left his 2CV in the Esplanade des Invalides underground car park, Monsieur Pamplemousse set off across the Rue Fabert with Pommes Frites at his side, mentally bracing himself for his coming encounter with the Director.

Véronique seemed unusually subdued when he arrived on the top floor of *Le Guide's* offices. 'I've no idea what's up,' she whispered as she opened the door to the holy of holies, 'but whatever it is – *bonne chance!*'

Briefly crossing himself as he entered the room, Monsieur Pamplemousse was just in time to catch the Director doing exactly the same thing behind his desk. Both hastily converted the movement into a tug of their right ear.

It was not a good omen; nor was Pommes Frites slow in registering the fact that his water bowl wasn't in its usual place. Having looked round the room and drawn a blank, he assumed his phlegmatic expression and settled himself down on the floor to await developments. It seemed to him that his master might be in for a bad time.

It wasn't long in coming.

'What, Pamplemousse, is the meaning of this?' demanded Monsieur Leclercq, pointing to his desk.

'Alerted by your use of the word *estragon* on my voice mail, I arrived back from Vonnas this morning, not having had any *petit déjeuner* I might add, and what do I find awaiting me?'

Glancing down at the desk, Monsieur Pamplemousse caught sight of a half eaten *croissant* lying in the ashtray. All became clear. It was no wonder the Director was in a bad mood.

'It is a long time since I had the good fortune to visit Vonnas, Monsieur, but I still remember their *petit dejeuner;* the basket of assorted *brioches* still warm from the oven, not to mention the freshly squeezed fruit juice and the home-made *confiture*. It was a wonderful start to the day. I fear the *croissants* in our canteen bear little resemblance to those of Monsieur Georges Blanc. To have had to forego them is indeed a tragedy.'

The Director stared at him for all of fifteen seconds. 'Sometimes, Pamplemousse,' he said at last, 'and I say this more in sorrow than in anger, I think you live in a dream world. Would that you had the strength of mind to confine your fantasies to the upper reaches of the stratosphere where they belong, rather than act them out in real life.

'*Croissants*, good, bad, or indifferent are the last things on my mind.

'Yesterday morning, here in this very office, in good faith I unburdened myself. I told you things I have told no other person, not even my wife...

'Especially my wife...' he added hastily.

'And what happened? No sooner had I turned my back than you were off round to Madame Chavignol. Pommes Frites too! Your appetites whetted, neither of you could wait. You are each of you as bad as the other. What one doesn't think of, the other one does!'

'With respect, *Monsieur*, it was you who suggested we went there in the first instance.'

'Do not try to shift the blame, Pamplemousse,' boomed the Director. 'What took place while you were there is a prime example of history repeating itself.'

Pausing to shift the ashtray, he picked up a sheaf of glossy photographs and held them aloft.

'Véronique informs me these were delivered early this morning by an oriental gentleman who refused to leave his name. He was under strict instructions to deliver them to me personally. It was only with great difficulty, and because I was late arriving, that she persuaded him otherwise. Fortunately he relented after she had given her word that no one else would open the package.

'How Madame Chavignol knew you worked for *Le Guide*, goodness only knows.'

Monsieur Pamplemousse could have told him, but he wasn't going to. It was only while sitting in the Square Samuel-Rousseau he realised to his dismay that in his haste to escape Claudette's clutches he had left his notebook on her bathroom radiator. Fortunately the notes were of no value to anyone else for they were written in his own particular form of shorthand. However, it had *Le Guide's* address in the front for return in case of loss. It wouldn't have taken her more than a moment to put two and two together.

'It is *pas grave*, Monsieur,' he said, trying to make light of it.

'Pas grave?' repeated the Director. *'Pas grave?* It is little short of a *catastrophe*! These photographs are worse, far worse than the ones Pommes Frites took of you earlier in the year with that Russian school-teacher on the Antibes peninsular. They make that particular occasion look like a school outing.'

'I suppose,' said Monsieur Pamplemousse thoughtfully, 'in a sense that's what it was.'

'At least in those you were not shown *sans vêtements,'* boomed the Director. 'As I recall you were still wearing your trousers. If any of these pictures were to fall into the hands of the media who knows what will happen? They will have a field day.'

Monsieur Pamplemousse shifted uneasily in his chair as he tried to get a glimpse of the photographs. All he could see was the ominous word *COPIE* stamped on the back of each one in red.

'But there was no one else present, *Monsieur*. Unlike your own unhappy experience with Madame Chavignol in the wash-house, flash guns were conspicuous by their absence.'

'Please don't remind me, Pamplemousse,' said Monsieur Leclercq. 'Every time I drive past a *laverie automatique* it all comes flooding back to me. I have tried varying my route into the office, but they are everywhere. Paris seems to be full of them. Does no one send their washing to a *blanchisserie* any more?'

'Only those who can afford it,' said Monsieur Pamplemousse pointedly. It was like water off a duck's back.

'In any case,' continued the Director, 'if what you say is true, how do you account for these?' He passed the photographs across his desk. 'They look as though whoever took them was using a *camera obscura*. A singularly ill-named device since most of your salient parts are far from *obscur*. They stand out a mile in fact!'

'It is kind of you to say so, *Monsieur*!'

Monsieur Leclercq controlled himself with difficulty. 'This is no time for levity, Pamplemousse. You know perfectly well what I mean.'

Going through the pictures Monsieur Pamplemousse could see the Director had a point. The shadowy nature of the shots and the lack of definition meant only one thing; they had been taken by closed-circuit video cameras.

Viewed in sequence they provided a visual record of all that had happened from the moment he entered the bathroom to Pommes Frites' arrival on the scene and beyond. The place must be alive with cameras. It also explained why the eyes in the painting had been pointing in different directions.

'The one exception,' said Monsieur Leclercq, 'is a group shot of you all lying in a heap on the floor. It appears to have been specially lit for the occasion.'

'That can be explained, *Monsieur*. When I first saw Madame Chavignol in a state of *déshabillage* I was so taken by surprise my feet became entangled with the flex on her bedside lamp and in my rush to escape her clutches it fell to the floor.'

The Director eyed him sceptically. 'You are sure it wasn't the other way round, Pamplemousse? You weren't bounding to her side?'

'Quite sure, *Monsieur*,' said Monsieur Pamplemousse virtuously. 'It was the last thing on my mind.'

'And the photograph you are holding in your hand,' boomed the Director. 'Why does that one appear to have been taken in some kind of rain storm?'

'In a sense it was, *Monsieur*. The carpet in Madame Chavignol's bedroom has – or rather *had – an* unusually thick pile, and in the course of time the inevitable happened. The heat from the lamp caused it to smoulder, and that in turn activated the sprinklers...'

Monsieur Leclercq sat in silence for a while, trying to picture it all. 'It wasn't your day, Aristide,' he said at last.

Holding out his hand for the photographs, he flipped through them again.

'Pommes Frites appears to be carrying out his task with unseemly relish,' he said. 'When he first appears on the scene he looks as though he is joining you in what I believe is known in some circles as a "gang bang", although what other term might be appropriate in the circumstances is hard to imagine.'

'He was coming to my rescue, *Monsieur*. After all, it is not for nothing that during his time in the *Sûreté* he was awarded the Pierre Armand Golden Bone Trophy for being sniffer dog of the year.'

'I hope it wasn't for doing what he appears to be doing in this picture,' said the Director severely. He held up one of the photographs. 'I assume Madame Chavignol did not offer the *Sûreté* her *derrière* for test purposes.'

'Indeed not, *Monsieur*. I think on this occasion it was more in the nature of a preliminary reconnaissance.'

'He certainly seems to be taking his time over it,' said the Director, removing another photograph from the pile. 'He's still at it in this one.'

'Pommes Frites is a perfectionist,' said Monsieur Pamplemousse proudly. 'It is the same with everything he does. When it comes to helping others he is possessed of an inexhaustible supply of goodwill. Nothing is too much trouble. I think he was upset that he might have bitten Madame Chavignol's *derrière* too hard by mistake. He was about to lick it better.'

'Hmmm,' said the Director sceptically. 'He does seem to

have a predilection for peoples' nether regions. It is no wonder his eyes are permanently blood-shot. In any case, what was her naked *derrière* doing pointing towards the ceiling in the first place? It was asking for trouble.'

'You can't really blame Pommes Frites,' said Monsieur Pamplemousse. 'It is in the nature of dogs. To them it is not unlike going behind the scenes at a theatre. Only there do you see the truth behind the masquerade.'

'It is a good job we don't all subscribe to that theory, Pamplemousse,' said the Director. 'I shudder to think what the streets of Paris would be like if we did. It is bad enough driving through the Bois de Boulogne at night...'

'He was doing it with the best of intentions, *Monsieur*. If he hadn't been there to defend me who knows what might have happened?'

The Director glanced down at the floor and as he did so his gaze softened.

'You are right, Aristide. Pommes Frites is a true friend and he has many fine qualities. Not only is he incorruptible and unflinching in the face of danger, but unlike many humans he is completely without guile. His heart is in the right place. There are times when I envy him his simple approach to life.'

Sensing the worst was over Pommes Frites sat up and wagged his tail.

The Director turned to Monsieur Pamplemousse. 'What are we to do, Aristide?

'Leave it to me, *Monsieur*. I will set the ball rolling in other quarters.'

Monsieur Leclercq visibly brightened. 'I knew you wouldn't let me down, Aristide. All I ask is that you remember our motto – the three A's. I trust you to place special regard to the last of them – *Anonymat*. If any of this were to get out it could mean curtains for us all.'

As they took their leave Monsieur Pamplemousse wondered if mentioning the delicious meal he'd had with Claudette would take the Director's mind off the matter. The possibility of finding a new star in the ascendancy for a future edition of *Le Guide* might cheer him up. He decided to save it until later. There was a time and place for everything.

Parking near the Quai des Orfèvres wasn't easy, but then it never had been. Finding a space at long last in the Place Dauphine, Monsieur Pamplemousse let Pommes Frites out for a run in the tiny Square du Vert Galant before going any further.

Waiting for him at the top of the steps, he gave an involuntary shiver. Despite the reflection of the sun's rays off the golden dome of the Institut de France further along the Seine, he could feel the first hint of autumn in the air. The leaves on the chestnut trees in the square were already beginning to turn.

But then, that corner of the Île de la Cité and the Conciergerie in particular, invariably struck a chill. Apart from Sainte Chapelle, with its stained glass windows, the centuries old buildings never lost their feeling of underlying menace. Today was no exception. They somehow underlined the Director's words; adding weight to his worst fears.

The ghost of Marie-Antoinette still lived on in the Palais de Justice, as did the ghosts of many others who had been incarcerated within its walls over the years. In the days before the revolution no one had been safe. It had been the police chief Sartine's proud boast that "whenever three people speak to each other in the street, one of them will be mine." During the Reign of Terror "justice" had been dispensed with the unremitting regularity of a *supermarché* check out.

It had spawned its own vocabulary too; some of the phrases still existed to this very day. The interrogation room, also known as *la chambre des aveux spontanés* – the voluntary confession room, was still called *la cuisine* by some. Instead of spilling the beans as a criminal in America might do under pressure, suspects were seated at a table where they "ate the morsel". *Il se met à table et mange le morceau*. It was a variation of what had gone on in the oldest tower of the Conciergerie, la tour Bonbec; the "tower of the heart eater" – the one who tells the cops what they want to hear.

None of the 2,500 or so citizens carted off to the guillotine by the tumbrel between the beginning of 1793 and July 1794 could have dreamed that one day the Conciergerie would become a tourist attraction; still less could they have pictured people actually going there of an evening to attend concerts and wine tastings.

Pommes Frites was clearly feeling the effect too. Peering gloomily at the waters of the Seine as a *Bâteau Mouche* went past at a rate of knots, he was rewarded by a burst of waving from the upper deck. One of the passengers threw him the end of a baguette, but it fell short and was carried away in the wash, so he hurried back to join his master.

Together they made their way to No 36 – the entrance to the *Police Judiciare*.

Once past the guard in his perspex box, they were soon in the thick of things and the mood passed. It was a long time since their last visit and it was worse than going back to *Le Guide's* offices after a tour in the provinces. There was so much handshaking and reminiscing it was some while before they reached the second floor.

The first big change Monsieur Pamplemousse noticed was that the Homicide Squad had become computerised with a vengeance. There were light grey boxes and screens everywhere.

'Aristide,' Jacques jumped to his feet as they entered his office. 'And Pommes Frites! *Ca va*?'

'*Bien, merci. Et vous*?'

Handshakes exchanged, backs patted, Jacques pulled up a chair for his guest and then resumed his own seat behind the desk.

'You look good – both of you. Don't say it – I've put on weight!' Caressing his stomach, he pointed to the screen. 'That's what comes of being wedded to a V.D.U.'

Monsieur Pamplemousse also noted Jacques was having trouble with his collar size. Normally a natty dresser, the top button of his shirt was undone and the tie halfway to being discarded altogether.

'Times change,' he said, 'and there's no going back.'

'More's the pity,' said Jacques. 'You know what they say... to err is human, but to really foul things up you need a computer.

'It's a wonderful tool. But that's all it is – a tool. If you're here to tell me someone has just driven into the back of your car and you can give me his number, in less time than it takes to say *sacré bleu* I'll be able to tell you all you need to know about the owner; where he lives, where he was born. On the other hand it won't tell me who was at the wheel.

'Ask any author. It's better than all the pens and pencils, but it still doesn't write books. As for saving paper...' He pointed to his IN tray. 'They don't come with a manual any more. You have to print the instructions out yourself. It must save the makers a fortune in Euros.'

Moving the mouse, Jacques stabbed at one of the keys and the computer emitted a shriek. It was followed in quick succession by a crash and the sound of an ambulance siren.

'Two hundred and eight since nine o'clock.' Jacques rubbed his hands together. 'Not a bad morning's work.'

'It's good to see you are keeping the flag flying,' said Monsieur Pamplemousse.

'*Comme d'habitude,*' said Jacques cheerfully. He swivelled the slim-line screen round to face them. 'It's the latest craze. You have to see how many pedestrians you can knock down in a given time.

'It used to be a Screen Saver. Then one of the backroom boys got to work modifying it. He's thinking of going commercial.

'I struck lucky soon after I came in this morning. There was this English tourist bus. It stopped on the Champs Élysées of all places to drop off the passengers. Drop off is right. They all got out the wrong side and went down like flies. Mind you, if it had been anywhere near a crossing I could have scored double!

'Ten points for anyone on a pedestrian crossing. Fifteen if they have a pushchair.'

'How about someone with a white stick?'

Jacques stared at him. 'Are you sick or something? It isn't that easy. Do that and you lose ten points. If they have a guide dog that's the end of the game.'

'Isn't having a Sheridan tank equipped with armour-piercing weaponry weighing the odds a bit in your favour?' persisted Monsieur Pamplemousse.

'Not at all,' said Jacques defensively. 'It's every man for himself in this world.

'Anyway, you must admit it's better than getting hooked on games like Freecell. That's what happened when we first got computerised. Everyone started reporting sick with eyestrain. I can't tell you the number of man-hours we lost.

'So...' He returned the screen to its normal position. 'I

take it you are not here because someone tried to climb up your exhaust pipe, but to talk about the demise of our late friend, Monsieur Claude Chavignol.'

'Any news?' Monsieur Pamplemousse felt it was high time he tested the water. 'If it's easier out of the office perhaps you could fill me in over a lunch. That is if you can tear yourself away from mowing down innocent pedestrians.'

Jacques looked at his watch. 'I'm rapidly coming the conclusion there is no such animal. Anyway, perhaps it's better if we talk up here. If you fancy a sandwich I'll have some sent up.'

'From the bar in the Place Dauphine?'

'Where else?' He picked up a phone.

'In that case,' said Monsieur Pamplemousse, 'tell them I'll have the usual.'

'There is, shall we say,' continued Jacques, as he completed the order, 'a certain apathy towards the case from on high. The consensus of opinion seems to be that whoever was responsible for Chavignol's death not only did everyone here a good turn, but they saved the taxpayer and the government a mint of money into the bargain, so why rock the boat? There are even those who say he... or maybe she... ought to be given the *Légion d'Honneur*...'

She? Monsieur Pamplemousse wondered. Statistically poison was more of a woman's method.

'Mind you, the boys in the vice squad are not best pleased. The truth of the matter is he'd been skating on their thin ice for a long time. The *Brigade Mondaine* has been building up a sizeable dossier and they were all set to pounce. They would have preferred to see him sent down for a good long stretch. *Alors*...

'It was one thing when it was a case of consenting adults. Who cares what people do in their spare time – just so long as they keep it to themselves? But when it became a case of lock up your small daughters or your sons it was something else again. With some people sex is like a drug. The more they get the more they want. And the more they have the more they start looking around for some new sensation. They say even the Chavignol's cat has left home with its tail between its legs.'

'The mind boggles.'

'The other day,' said Jacques, 'I read of an English train stopping somewhere in an isolated part of the country, and the passengers were treated to the spectacle of a farmer having it off with a goat would you believe?'

'Ah, *les anglais*! Nothing defeats them!'

'It pays not to turn your back on them,' said Jacques darkly. 'Anyway, with all those witnesses you'd think it was an open and shut case.'

'And?'

'He was let off with a caution. The police went to interview the goat and reported that it seemed perfectly happy. Their recommendation was that the passengers on the train be given counselling.'

'So? What is the connection?'

Jacques gave the classic see-saw motion with his right hand. 'Because, and you know it as well as I do, things are never quite what they seem. To put it bluntly, as far as Chavignol is concerned there are those in high places not a million kilometres away who will sleep easier in their beds if a line can be drawn under the whole affair as of now. Look into it too deeply and you could be opening up a whole can of worms.

'Anyway, apart from being there when it happened, what's your interest in the matter? I see you had your photograph in this morning's *journaux* again. Watering your herbs on the balcony this time.'

Monsieur Pamplemousse made a face. 'Let us just say there are people – some of whom I happen to know are perfectly innocent – who are having sleepless nights over certain photographs that would be better destroyed. And I don't mean that one.'

Jacques shrugged. 'I assumed as much. It is what I have heard too. But they could be anywhere ... a safe deposit box ... a bank vault ... buried in the garden... who knows? Start any kind of search involving too many people and the media will be on to it like a shot. Once they smell a rat there's no knowing where it will end.'

'I know where they may be kept,' said Monsieur Pamplemousse.

'You do?' Jacques was suddenly all attention.

'There is a safe in Madame Chavignol's bedroom. Quite a sophisticated one.'

'I won't ask how you know.'

'I wouldn't tell you if you did,' said Monsieur Pamplemousse. 'Not for the moment anyway, but it would be good to see inside it...' He broke off as there was a knock at the door.

'*Entrez!*' called Jacques.

An elderly waiter entered carrying a tray above his shoulder. His face lit up at the sight of Jacques' visitor.

'Monsieur Pamplemousse!' He could hardly contain his excitement as he put the tray down. 'I saw you on television the other night. It was on in the bar. *And* I saw your picture in all the *journaux*. It is a long time since that happened.

'Remember all that nonsense about those girls at the *Folies*? So what if you did take some photographs of them through a hole in the ceiling? I remember saying to the wife – I doubt if the girls themselves cared two shakes of a fan dancer's feather.'

107

Monsieur Pamplemousse wondered if he would ever be allowed to forget the episode. 'Someone had it in for me.'

'As for that Chavignol...' The waiter placed the tray on the Jacques' desk. 'Him and his rug. My wife always says never trust a man who wears a toupee. She reckons he must have something to hide.'

Monsieur Pamplemousse was tempted to suggest it could be a bald patch, but he let it go.

'Did you know Chavignol had a toupee?' asked Jacques, when the waiter had gone.

Monsieur Pamplemousse shook his head. He had been as close to him as anyone and he certainly hadn't spotted it. But then, his mind had been on other things.

'Trust a woman to notice.' Jacques opened a desk drawer and took out two Paris goblets, along with a couple of napkins and some plates.

Monsieur Pamplemousse eyed the tray as he tucked one of the napkins under his chin: two lengths of *baguette* split down the middle, with ham, lettuce, tomato and mayonnaise folded in. Two *barquettes aux framboises*. A *pichet* of Côtes de Rhône. He gave a sigh of contentment. *Parfait* was the only word for it.

He reached for the nearest *baguette*. It was fresh from the second baking of the day; crisp and slightly warm to the touch. Breaking a piece off the end he handed it to Pommes Frites. It made up for the one he had missed.

Jacques set about pouring the wine. 'I hope you don't mind my saying so, but given that photographs are involved, it does sound a bit like history repeating itself.'

'There are certain similarities,' admitted Monsieur Pamplemousse.

When the photograph, supposedly taken by him through a hole drilled in the ceiling of the changing room at the *Folies* first surfaced he'd thought it was some kind of joke, but as other bits of planted evidence began to appear he knew better.

Normally it would have passed unremarked, but it so happened it not only coincided with the "silly season" in the newspaper world, but also at a time when the press were gunning for the police. They'd had a field day. Resignations were called for. Fed up with it all he had taken early retirement.

Then one day he had bumped into Monsieur Leclercq who had offered him a job on the spot, since when he had never looked back. Another example of coincidence at work, or had that, too, been meant?

'The question is how to make sure these particular photographs are destroyed before they fall into the wrong hands,' he said. 'That really would be history repeating itself.'

'If you're thinking of a breaking and entering job,' said Jacques, 'don't look at me. I'd have my work cut out selling that idea upstairs.

'If we didn't get it right first time the examining magistrate would be down on us like a ton of bricks. That's not to say a little bit of private enterprise would be amiss. It would certainly be quicker in the long run – and safer.'

'In other words, I'm on my own.'

'Not necessarily; at least, not entirely. I could guarantee a certain amount of co-operation.'

'The place is riddled with security,' said Monsieur Pamplemousse. 'Video cameras inside and out ... gates at all the windows ... state of the art door fittings... you name it. It's worse than Fort Knox.'

'It isn't for me to suggest names,' said Jacques. 'You know them as well as I do. But it sounds like a job for Malfiltre. Just up his street in fact. They don't come more enterprising and *privé* could be his middle name.'

'He's still in his old job?' Lowering his voice, Monsieur Pamplemousse named one of the grander security firms in Paris.

'The last time I heard he was their chief advisor. I think he probably pays them for the privilege. He might even have had a hand in designing the Chavignols' system. You never know your luck.'

'What would be in it for him?'

'He owes us one,' said Jacques. 'In fact, you might say he's permanently in our debt. Freedom is a very precious commodity.'

'Same guarantees?

'Turning a blind eye can be habit-forming. Besides, he's much more use to us where he is instead of being behind bars. I can give you his number if you like.'

Jacques reached for a pen and pad.

'How about the shells I sent you?'

'They're with forensic now.'

'No prints other than Chavignol's?'

Jacques gave a groan. 'You must be joking. Have you ever tried getting prints off an oyster shell? France alone farms around 2,000 million a year and I doubt if you would get one usable print off the lot.

'Anyway, it could have been done some time before. The *spéciales de claire* will stay fresh for anything up to ten days. And even if it had been opened, an oyster can close up again if it's left. That apart, the poison could have been injected with the aid of a syringe.'

Helping himself to a *barquette*, Monsieur Pamplemousse held it up to the light. The *pâte sucrée* pastry shell had a little *crème pâtissière* in the bottom and the raspberries had been given a light redcurrant jelly glaze; a classic combination. He took a bite.

'Good?'

'*Superbe*! Just as I remember them.'

'Don't forget,' said Jacques, 'we haven't spoken, but I shall be waiting to hear.'

'Good luck in the meantime,' said Monsieur Pamplemousse drily, nodding at the screen.

'You don't think I'm doing this for fun, do you?' said Jacques. 'It's quality thinking time. It helps concentrate the mind. Based on my researches, I've been compiling a mental list of all the people who might have wanted Chavignol out of the way. It adds up to nearly as many as my score of pedestrians.

'Have you still got your old 2CV?' he asked, apropos of nothing.

Monsieur Pamplemousse nodded.

'You realise that if it had been developed by the software industry you would have been able to get a new one for the price of a good meal by now, and it would have done 500 kilometres to the litre.'

'I know,' said Monsieur Pamplemousse. 'But it would have crashed twice a day for no apparent reason, and if you pressed the Help button it would have told you to reinstall the engine. I shall stick to my old one, thank you very much.'

'*Touché*!' Jacques returned to his keyboard. 'I'll be in touch if I get any news.'

Good though it had been to see Jacques, it was a relief to be out in the fresh air again. Taking in the timelessness of it all as he strolled past the *bouquinistes* lining the banks of the Seine, Monsieur Pamplemousse found himself wondering what difference it would have made if computers had been around in the days of the Revolution. Not a lot probably, except that everything would have taken much longer. The police had always been bogged down with paperwork, and that was especially true now they were computerised.

It was time to follow up his next line of approach. Tomorrow would do. He'd had more than enough for one day.

Chapter Six

It was Monsieur Pamplemousse's favourite time of the day; the few hours in the morning when Montmartre belonged to those who lived there. Not only was the Place du Tertre free of "artists" touting for custom, but it was even possible to see the steps leading up to the Sacré-Coeur from as far away as the Square Willette at the bottom of the hill.

In short, you could walk wherever you wanted to without bumping into hordes of tourists searching for things they would never find.

There had been an improvement since coaches were made to disgorge their passengers in the Boulevard Rochechouart to the south of the hill, but he and Doucette still occasionally talked of moving to somewhere less crowded and more convenient.

Every time an old *boulangerie* or a fruit and vegetable shop gave up the fight, only to be replaced by a chic boutique or a souvenir shop full of tiny Eiffel Towers and snowstorm models of the Sacré-Coeur, the subject came up again.

If it hadn't been for the little Montmartrobus that stopped almost outside their apartment block, they might well have done so by now.

It was a switchback of a journey, full of hazards: driving at speed through gaps with barely a centimetre or so to spare on either side; travelling a half kilometre or more to cover what to a crow would have been less than a hundred metres. There was never a dull moment. But it did mean Doucette could do her shopping either in the Rue Lepic at one end of its run, or the Rue Ordener at the other, with the added bonus of a guaranteed seat on the way home.

But having said that, he had to admit he would miss the view across the rooftops of Paris from their balcony. The apartment was only a stone's throw from the Moulin de la Galette, one-time haunt of Renoir and Toulouse-Lautrec. Further up the hill, where the Rue Norvin joined the Rue des Saules, the scene in the early morning was much as it had been when Utrillo first painted it.

There was certainly a village atmosphere at the start of the day; locals exchanging greetings as they went about their business, sparrows taking advantage of clean water flowing down the gutters for a quick bathe while they could, restaurants laying out their tables for lunch, and not least, the streets leading down to the Boulevard de Clichy on the south side were briefly devoid of prostitutes and their pimps.

Following his usual route, Monsieur Pamplemousse cut through the Rue d'Orchamp and led the way downhill via the Place Émile-Goudeau, site of the old Bâteau Lavoir where Picasso and others had turned the world of art upside down.

On reaching the Place des Abbesses he bought a copy of *Le Parisien*, checked the day's weather: imperturbable, but watch out for storms later; then retraced his steps a short distance before branching off and heading north-west-wards towards the *Centre de Télévision et Ciné de la Butte*.

He wondered what he would find when he got there.

Jacques was right, of course. By all accounts there must be a good many people who wouldn't have minded seeing Chavignol dead. But wishing someone dead was a far cry from actually carrying out the deed in cold blood. Besides, why choose such a spectacular way of going about it? It was almost as if whoever was responsible wanted to make sure it was witnessed by as many people as possible. If that were the case, they had certainly achieved their objective.

Pausing only to leave his mark on the *Belle Époque* entrance to the Metro, Pommes Frites followed on behind, keeping a watchful eye on his master who was clearly in a thoughtful mood and not to be trusted on his own.

Turning a corner, they both had to leap for their lives as a small white van bearing the film company's logo shot past at speed, the driver hunched over the wheel.

In trying to avoid cannoning into a meter maid, hovering on the pavement pencil in hand, Monsieur Pamplemousse made a grab for the wing mirror of a tiny Smart car parked sideways on between two bollards. The air was suddenly filled with a cacophony of sound; a horn going full blast, a dog barking its head off.

'*Oh, la, la!*' An elderly lady with a shopping basket on wheels crossed herself. Two cats asleep on the roof of the car leapt into the air and made a bolt for it as though their end was nigh.

Pommes Frites gave them a withering look as they shot up an alleyway. It wasn't as though the barking was real. It was simply the meaningless hodge-podge of noise some cars made when they were pushed. Something any self-respecting dog would know without being told.

Monsieur Pamplemousse stared after the van as it disappeared round another corner. It was probably nothing more than an association of ideas – the driver's face had been partly obscured by a wide-brimmed hat – but if he hadn't known better he would have sworn it was Monsieur Chavignol himself at the wheel. The impious notion entered his mind that perhaps having found the Pearly Gates closed he was hurrying to be first in the queue elsewhere.

The *periwinkle* began writing in her book. He didn't stop to ask her if she was recording the number of the van or the parked car; perhaps it was both.

Gates of a more mundane kind further along the street were also closed. Having presented his card to the commissionaire and stated his business, he waited while the man made a telephone call.

The spot normally occupied by the Facel Vega was taken up by a large scenery van. It could be why it had been moved so quickly – space must be at a premium.

Life seemed to be carrying on as usual. It might have been a country inn anywhere in France; the staff getting ready for lunch instead of making films. Pools of water below the window boxes showed they had only recently been watered. Drawn curtains across some upper floor windows at the far end of the courtyard were the only sign that anything untoward had taken place.

There had been a period in the seventies when whole areas had been razed to the ground with the brutal relentlessness of a Baron Haussman, but without his vision of a Grand Plan. Now it was a case of façades being preserved, while the buildings behind them were gutted and reshaped to meet modern needs. At least it meant it was possible to enjoy the best of both worlds.

He came back down to earth as the gates swung open automatically and an elegantly dressed black girl appeared and handed him a tag with his name in large type to clip on his lapel. Having produced a second blank one for Pommes Frites, she thought better of it and motioned them to follow her.

As she led the way along a corridor Monsieur Pamplemousse was struck by the informality of it all; each office they passed seemed to be decorated in a different style according the occupant's place in the scheme of things. Cardboard models of sets were on display in the office of the Head of Designs. Head of Make-up had chosen to fill the room with wigs on display stands. The Head of Engineering had an antique illuminated neon sign on the wall advertising DUBONNET.

Only the door marked Head of Accounts was shut. The muted strains of Wagner's *Tristan and Isolde*, written at a time when he, too, was having trouble balancing the books, probably reflected the mood inside.

The room Monsieur Pamplemousse eventually found himself ushered into was larger than the others. Apart from a "La Pavoni" coffee machine on a table in one corner, it was filled with antiques: an assortment of hunter watches in a glass-fronted display case on one wall, clocks galore on the other three. They were interspersed with mounted heads of animals he didn't immediately recognise.

Pommes Frites eyed the latter nervously as he followed on behind.

At first sight Monsieur Pamplemousse mistook the person behind the desk for a cleaner using the office phone while the boss was out of the room. A half empty coffee cup, a black armband and an unlit cigar clenched between the teeth – temporarily removed while its owner motioned him to take a seat – put him straight.

'Ramonacatspullupachair.'

It struck him forcibly that the holder of the post fulfilled all current P.C. requirements in one fell swoop. Short, fat, black, New York Jewish if he was any judge of accents, a dyed ginger wig which looked as though it wasn't on straight, a tattooed symbol of the European Union on the right forearm: no section of the community could have had cause for complaint, unless you happened to be tall, white, and a French male.

Prominently displayed in front of a bank of telephones, the name on an elongated triangular desk plate facing the door – *Ramona D. Katz. Directeur Général* – left him in no doubt as to whom he was addressing.

She caught him looking at it as she replaced the receiver. 'I know what you're thinking. My father had Spanish blood in him. I don't know from where. You tell me.'

'Call me Randy. Everyone else around here does.'

It was like listening to a talking machine gun. 'Randy...' Monsieur Pamplemousse nervously tried it out.

'Don't I know you from somewhere?' As she rose to her feet, hand outstretched, he realised he'd hardly noticed the difference. Given the cigar, he was irresistibly reminded of Monsieur Bibendum: short, round, amply endowed with rolls of flesh, but without the inevitable glass of champagne *Le Guide's* pre-war arch rival was always holding in those days.

What he did notice was a warm draught of hot air as she leant towards him. It was the nearest thing to a stink bomb from his childhood. Even Pommes Frites blinked twice before retreating to a far corner of the room. Monsieur Pamplemousse hastily sat down and began explaining the purpose of his visit.

'Scumbag!'

Seeing the startled look on his face, she removed the cigar again and using the end of it as a pointer directed his attention towards a photograph on the wall. 'Not you... him!'

'You did not like Monsieur Chavignol, *Mademoiselle*?' Monsieur Pamplemousse hazarded a guess at her marital status. Given her world-class halitosis, no man could possibly share a bed with her and live to tell the tale.

'Does the Pope like bagels?'

'I have no idea,' admitted Monsieur Pamplemousse.

'But if you really disliked him so much, why are you here?'

'Why do you do what you do?' came the reply.

'Because I don't know anything else and because I happen to enjoy it,' was the simple answer.

'Right! Me? I work here because it keeps me in the style I've grown accustomed to. Can you think of a better reason?

'You know something? I didn't kill Chavignol if that's what you're thinking! I worked hard to get where I am. You think I want to throw it all away?

'I tell you something else about him. He may have been a schmuck, but he made life easy for me. He could plant product the way nobody else could. I'll give you an example.'

She tilted her chair so far back Monsieur Pamplemousse was worried it might topple over carrying her with it. Worse still, as her skirt rode up he wondered if she was about to put her feet on the desk. Alarmed at the thought, he averted his gaze, concentrating instead on a wall cabinet filled with antique objects, some of which he didn't immediately recognise.

'Got it in one! Potato peelers. Remember the item he did on them?' Monsieur Pamplemousse didn't, but then neither did he want to interrupt the flow of information.

'The day after that programme was aired sales went up over 500%. They disappeared off the shelves. All over France! It's what's known as the "Chavignol Effect". It got to the stage if he was going to mention something – anything – we had to send out an advance warning to the trade. Coffee makers, tinned herrings, ice cream, knives ... you name it. You want to know why? Because he had authority. People listened to him.'

'Was he paid by the manufacturers?'

'Did I say that? I tell you, he was a one-off. He's going to be missed.'

It struck Monsieur Pamplemousse that it was time to redress the balance a little. Ignoring the possibility that it could be fatal, he took a deep breath and set out to list a few of Claude Chavignol's faults. 'From all I have heard...'

'Listen!' Mademoiselle Katz held up her hands. 'You don't have to tell me.

'So what? Nobody's perfect. When you got something that works you go with it. In this business we're all cogs. Big ones ... little ones. We depend on each other. It just so happens we've lost the biggest cog of all – the king-size one that drove all the others. That he should do this to me!'

'Bad luck!' Monsieur Pamplemousse tried to sound more sympathetic than he felt.

'Bad luck?' Mademoiselle Katz shrugged. 'Even for bad luck you need luck. But I tell you,' she tapped her forehead. 'I need this piece of shit hitting the fan like I need a hole in my *kop*.'

Dipping into a large open confectionery jar she removed what appeared to be a whole baklava and stuffed it into her mouth.

Monsieur Pamplemousse had difficulty deciphering her next remark. He made a stab at it.

'How can you help?' he repeated. 'I'd like to look around, if I may. Get the feel of what actually happened the other evening.'

'You want the Grand Tour, huh? I'd do it myself, but I got problems with my problems. There's a big gap in the schedule and nobody to fill it. We gotta to move fast.'

Reaching out, she picked up a telephone receiver.

'Jules? I have a *goy* here by the name of Grapefruit... Yeah. The very same... I want you to drop everything and take him on a guided tour. Show him anything he wants to see. Right...'

A second phone rang, then a third. Fastening the first under her chin she began juggling the other two, barking orders into first one, then the other.

Noting that she ended up putting the second phone back on the wrong cradle just as a fourth one rang, it struck Monsieur Pamplemousse that if the studios were looking for an act to replace Claude Chavignol they need look no further.

He felt a hand on his shoulder.

'Don't worry,' murmured the newcomer as he ushered them out of the office. 'They don't all work. It's Randy's way of terminating a conversation. Never fails.'

He held out his hand. 'The name's Julian. Julian House – Head of Production. Or, perhaps I should use the past tense. I'm not sure what's going to happen now.'

Monsieur Pamplemousse glanced back over his shoulder to say goodbye and immediately wished he hadn't. Mademoiselle Katz was putting her feet up at last.

He followed the other back down the corridor. 'Sorry to rush you,' said Julian, 'but it's nearly eleven o'clock and all hell breaks loose in her office when the clocks start striking.'

He glanced down at Pommes Frites padding along behind them. 'If you don't mind, I think we'd better leave him somewhere safe for the time being. Dogs are strictly *verboten* in the studios. Unless he happens to be carrying a union card.'

'How did she get to be where she is?' asked Monsieur Pamplemousse.

'Ramona? She arrived before my time. She does seem a bit unreal when you first meet her. If you ask me she had something on our late lamented boss. Don't ask me what or from where, but she had something.'

Monsieur Pamplemousse couldn't help feeling relieved. It meant there was some justice in the world after all.

'Not that she isn't good at her job,' Julian hastened to add. 'Randy could sell snow ploughs to the Arabian government if she put her mind to it. She's O.K. really. Her breath's worse than her bite. The trouble is she suffers from an inferiority complex, which isn't surprising all things considered.'

Stopping by a small lift marked *PRIVÉ*, he inserted a key. 'I'll take you up to Claude Chavignol's old apartment. His "retreat". Your partner in crime will be safe there.'

As the doors slid open muted strains of the Count Basie trio playing their fast version of "Lady Be Good" emerged. Monsieur Pamplemousse stifled the protest he had been about to make. What was Basie's famous phrase? Jazz is four beats to the bar and no cheating. He lived by that.

Unsure of which way they were going, he waited until they were inside and Julian pressed the only button. The answer was in the same direction as the music – up.

'What will happen to the company now?' he asked.

'Who knows? It depends what arrangements have been made. It may need more than a smidgeon of creative accounting for a while, but that's par for the course in this business. Knowing Claude I imagine he will have had it all tied up.

'After you, chaps.'

As the lift came to a stop and the doors slid open, Julian stood back. Following them out, he crossed to the windows and drew the curtains, flooding the room with light.

Monsieur Pamplemousse registered the courtyard before taking in the room itself. Having already sampled the Chavignols' lifestyle at their home in the 7th, he was expecting more of the same, but it was the very opposite. The walls were hung with framed theatre posters: French,

122

American...there was even one from the Holborn Empire in London. They looked as though they were mostly from the immediate post-war years when Music Halls were fighting a losing battle with television.

A huge bowl of fresh flowers occupied a central position on a conference-size table. Beyond it, in a far corner of the room there was a theatrical dressing table, the mirror ringed with lights for make-up. The work surface was dotted with silver framed signed photographs of the great and the famous. On the wall to one side of it there was a framed reproduction of *The Conjurer* by Hieronymous Bosch.

It revealed another, more personal side to Chavignol and he wondered who in the end was the more dominant of the two, Claude or Claudette? It wouldn't surprise him if it were the latter. More dominant, and perhaps more dangerous.

'Impressed?' Julian joined him. 'You haven't seen anything yet. Claude didn't believe in stinting himself.'

He led the way past a fairground slot machine into a second room that had been converted into a viewing theatre. A row of leather armchair type seats, each with a projecting ring for holding a carton in one arm, occupied the nearside wall; a popcorn machine in a far corner was matched by a mini bar at the opposite end. Julian selected a button in a console set into one of the chair arms and curtains between the two parted to reveal a giant screen. Pressure on a second button sent shock waves of stereophonic music through the room.

Beyond the viewing theatre, a marble-floored area was home to Bulthaup steel kitchen cabinets and an Angelo Po oven and hob built into an island unit with a granite work surface.

Having beaten the others to it, Pommes Frites looked

round expectantly as they entered. Tongue hanging out, he was eyeing his reflection in the mirrored doors of a vast American General Electric fridge-freezer with built-in water and ice dispensers.

'He's welcome to some water,' said Julian, 'but I doubt if he'll find anything worthwhile to go with it.' Opening the door he pointed to a half-eaten pizza and a pack of Soothing Eye Masks. 'Take your pick!

'I'm afraid it does make a bit of a mockery of Claude's standing as a gourmet. The trouble was he had no taste-buds, and no sense of smell either. Which I suppose is why he didn't notice anything wrong with the oyster until it was too late.

'He had a Japanese chef who did the cooking here whenever he was entertaining – hence all the equipment. No mean hand at it either by all accounts.'

Monsieur Pamplemousse didn't let on he knew only too well. Instead, while the other went about filling a water bowl for Pommes Frites, he glanced at some of the labels on a hundred or so bottles behind a glass-fronted temperature controlled wine cabinet.

'For someone with no taste buds he didn't exactly stint himself.'

'He was guided entirely by the right hand column of the price lists,' said Julian. 'Which makes life easy if you can afford it.'

Pommes Frites looked up at the others. He had no idea what they were on about. Had they been engaged in a game of hunt the slipper they couldn't have been further off the scent. In fact – he gazed, glassy-eyed at the bowl of water in front of him – they were getting colder by the minute.

'Claude may not have been in the same league as Britney Spears,' said Julian, leading the way back to where they had started. 'Who else is on this side of the Atlantic? In fact, compared with most Hollywood film stars he was a non-starter, but in his own immodest way he didn't do too badly. Fresh flowers every day. A new suit from Cerruti before every show – they have his measurements on computer – all courtesy of the budget.'

Apart from making a mental calculation of what that would add up to over a thirteen-week series, Monsieur Pamplemousse listened with only half an ear as he ran his eye along the bookshelves. Books could say more about a person than almost anything else.

Unlike the ones in Chavignol's house they looked well used. Yellow marker tabs protruded from the pages and as with the posters, they appeared to be in an assortment of languages. Most had to do with illusions and the art of conjuring in one form or another; an English edition of Dunninger's *Complete Encyclopaedia of Magic*, and various other titles which meant nothing to him, apart from *The Expert at the Card Table* by someone called S.W.Erdnase. He wondered why that rang a bell. Perhaps Glandier had mentioned it at some time.

'The card sharp's bible,' said Julian. 'And therein lies the biggest mystery of all. Who actually wrote it? The theory is that S.W. Erdnase is a part-inversion of Andrews, who was a Massachusetts gambler, but that's as far as anyone has ever got for certain. He's another one who came to a sticky end. Except his was self-inflicted. When the San Francisco police finally caught up with him he shot the woman he was with, then committed suicide. '

'Never play poker with a professional,' said Monsieur Pamplemousse.

'I certainly wouldn't have wanted to take on Claude. He was never without a pack of cards. That's what it's all about. Practice, practice, practice. It's the Martina

Navratilova syndrome. They say she has tennis balls all over her house so that any time she goes into a room she can pick one up and squeeze it. Claude was the same with cards.

'Anyway, dealing from the bottom of the pack was only one of his many talents. When he first started out he worked with people like Kellar and Hermann in America before going solo. In his day he was a class act. Then, when magic went out of favour, he adapted his skills to new ends.'

'How old was he?'

Julian shrugged. 'Older than you think! Look, I don't want to disillusion you any more than you probably are already, but in this business age is no barrier. There are people who get wheeled on simply because their main, perhaps their only qualification, is the ability to move around a set without bumping into the furniture.

'Claude didn't come into that category – he knew exactly what he was doing. Every move was calculated to the nth degree. He also had most of the qualities that go with being a successful television presenter. He was unflappable and never at a loss for a word – even when there was nothing to say. In short, he was a born television host. The job could have been made for him.

'If television hadn't been invented it's hard to picture what he might have become. A card sharp perhaps, or a magician down on his luck, reduced to doing children's parties at Christmas. As it was he took to the small screen like a duck to water and he never looked back.'

'What was he like to work for?'

'The scene boys call him "the big cheese" behind his back.'

'*Le grand chavignol*? I know that syndrome too,' said Monsieur Pamplemousse, with feeling. 'The trouble is everyone thinks they are the only one to have thought of it.'

'In Claude's case it wasn't meant as a compliment. Think over-ripe Roquefort stinking to high heaven instead.'

'And you? What was your opinion?'

'Try poisoned honey. The fact is his whole life was devoted to the art of illusion. With most people what you see is what you get. With Claude it was the opposite. He was a product of his own invention. Being with him when he was at the wheel of his car was something else again. Beaming out at pedestrians in case anyone recognised him, and at the same time doing his best to mow them down. No one was safe.'

'Talking of which...' Monsieur Pamplemousse related his narrow escape on the way to the studios.

'That would have been Pascal,' said Julian. 'He's as bad behind the wheel, except in his case it isn't deliberate. He just isn't a very good driver. It's a bit ironic really. Only the other day Claude half jokingly promised to leave him his Facel Vega when he died.'

'Half?'

'More than half I would say. They've been together for years. Pascal is part of the fixtures and fittings you might say.' He pointed to one of the photographs on the dressing table.

Monsieur Pamplemousse took a closer look. Even given the fact that the person in the photograph was as bald as a coot and sported a toothbrush moustache, the likeness was uncanny. The only physical difference he could see lay in the hands, which were more those of a workman than a magician.

'That's him.'

'All part of the service,' said Julian, catching the look on

127

his face. 'I'm not surprised you were thrown. In the beginning I was caught out more than once. When he's wearing a hat it's hard to tell the two apart. It's like the old saying about pets and their masters growing to look like each other...present company excepted, of course, although rumour has it they were distantly related.'

'So he might have been here this morning?'

'Could be. He came and went all the time. Apart from being Claude's *coursier de production* – his "gofer" as it's known in the trade – "go for this – go for that", Pascal was his stand-in during camera rehearsals. It isn't unusual for a star to have someone do all the tedious work. It's what they call "saving themselves" for the night.'

'Why would he have come back?'

'He probably had things to pick up. It's a kind of home from home for him.'

'Presumably he would have checked in at the gate?'

'Not necessarily. The lift isn't the only way in. Fire regulations. There's a back entrance leading out to the Rue Tholozé. It came in useful the other night, I can tell you. There was quite a crowd waiting outside the main entrance.'

That explained why the *Sapeurs-Pompiers* had been heard but not seen; the ambulance and the police too.

'And Pascal would still have a key?'

'Almost certainly.'

'And the use of a company *camionnette*?'

'There's no reason why he shouldn't still be using it. As I say, he was Claude's Man Friday. All these things will need to be sorted out. It's early days yet.'

'It would be good to see him.'

'I don't have his number, but I'll get my secretary to tell him you called.'

'Did the two of them get on together?'

'Claude and Pascal? If they didn't it never showed. Although I didn't see much of them together.'

'And Madame Chavignol?'

'Between you, me and the gatepost, she wore the trousers. I wouldn't trust her any further than I could throw her. They were well matched.'

Julian looked as though he could have said a great deal more, but he changed his mind.

'Listen; let me take you down on the floor. They'll be rehearsing *Montparnasse Bienvenue*...' he named a twice-weekly soap opera, which Monsieur Pamplemousse had to admit he had never seen. 'It's our other bread and butter show. It'll be a different director, but the crew will be the same.'

The atmosphere and layout of the studio had changed completely since his last visit. The theatre with its proscenium arch and stage had disappeared, as had the audience rostra. The space was now completely taken up by sets – mostly three-walled rooms with one side left free for the technical staff to operate in. Through the window of one he could see the Montparnasse Tower painted on a backcloth; through another there was a view of the cemetery.

He recognised the floor manager, who looked up from his clipboard and gave him a wave.

On the surface it was the usual chaos, with everyone talking jargon: the lighting director holding a pencil vertically over his left hand, wondering whether or not to "Chinese" the barn door on a 2k; a boom operator towering above the others on a mobile platform trying to lose a microphone shadow; cameramen working out tracking lines and deciding which lenses to use as they marked up their crib cards; actors getting accustomed to their surroundings, testing door handles for size; studio hands coming and going, making sure props were in their right place, comparing their positioning with stock photos from previous episodes. A gardener was watering a row of practical plants just outside one of the windows; a scenic artist busied himself with a long handled brush, painting a floral carpet on the studio floor.

'Chaos with a capital K,' said Julian. 'It'll be all right on the night. It always is. Well, almost always.' He pointed to a steel staircase in a far corner of the studio. 'Let's go and see where it's all put together.'

Following on behind until they reached the gallery, Monsieur Pamplemousse listened while Julian House explained in a whisper what each of the monitors in a long row behind the vision mixer's desk was for.

The voice of an actor down in the studio querying the reason for his getting up and leaving the room came over the fold-back. It sounded as though it wasn't the first time.

'Tell him his mother's just died,' said the director unfeelingly. 'That'll motivate him!

'Actors!' he groaned, masking a desk microphone with his hand.

Looking round and recognising his visitors, he uncovered the microphone and spoke to the studio manager. 'Tell the cast to take five.'

Everyone in the gallery relaxed while Julian explained the purpose of their visit.

'Feel free,' said the director. 'I'm afraid I can't be much help. I go with this show, but I saw it all happen on the box at home. Shame you weren't able to catch Chavignol in time.'

'It would have needed a miracle,' said Monsieur Pamplemousse.

'That kind of miracle wouldn't come cheap,' said the director cryptically. 'Anyway, apart from my secretary, Désirée,' he gestured to a blonde girl sitting beside him, 'she calls the shots and generally keeps me in order, everyone else here was working on the show. Anne-Marie, the vision-mixer ...Didier, technical operations manager...' A wave toward a window beyond the monitors embraced the sound supervisor, 'Jean-Michel.' He glanced up at a wall clock. 'They're all yours, but I'd be grateful if it doesn't take too long, otherwise we shall start running out of time.'

'Isn't it unusual for a network to take a live feed for Chavignol's kind of programme?' asked Monsieur Pamplemousse.

'Unique,' replied Didier. 'Especially in this day and age.'

'On the other hand,' said Julian, 'it was one of the things that kept the viewing figures high. Human nature being what it is, viewers lived in hope that one day something might go wrong; a bit like people secretly wanting a trapeze artist to miss his footing.'

'In Chavignol's case they got their wish,' said the director drily.

'He was a perfectionist,' said Julian. 'He hated people to think his tricks were performed by sleight of TV. He believed they should be things of the moment.'

'How did he get away with it?' asked Monsieur Pamplemousse. 'Going out live, I mean.'

'Let's just say he had "friends" in high places,' said Julian. 'He could be very persuasive.'

'My understanding is that he wasn't very practical when it came to working in the kitchen.'

'He was paranoid about his hands. They were insured for God knows how much.'

'In that case,' said Monsieur Pamplemousse, 'wasn't it unusual for him to open the oyster himself? It isn't the easiest thing in the world.'

'You're right. But he was very insistent on doing it himself for once. I guess it was because there was only one. It was probably the magician in him. It would have offended his sense of drama.'

'Who supplied it?'

'He brought it in himself. He had his own chef at home. He supplied most of the dishes he used on the show.'

'As for opening it,' said Didier, 'I suspect it was helped on its way earlier. Although they do have a tendency to close up again.'

'We can check with the studio manager,' said Miles. 'But I agree. It must have been that way. Timing was everything with Claude. It has to be on a live show. There's no second chance. On the surface he made it seem as though he was skating on thin ice, but believe me that was very rarely the case.'

Memories of Chavignol's boiled egg still lingered in Monsieur Pamplemousse's mind. 'But there must have been times when it was touch and go,' he insisted, reminding the others of the moment.

'Don't you believe it,' said Didier. 'He had eyes like a hawk.'

'It's a very good example,' said Julian. 'When we go back down on the floor, have a look behind where last night's audience were sitting. You'll see a large clock with a sweep second hand high up on the wall. It was kept covered up for most of the show. Unbeknown to them he knew exactly how long he had.'

'If everything was so cut and dried,' said Monsieur Pamplemousse thoughtfully, 'it must have come as even more of a shock when he keeled over like he did.'

'Panic stations,' said the vision mixer. 'If you are wondering why the programme wasn't faded at once, it's because the ball was in the network's court. It was only a matter of seconds, but in this business a second can seem like an eternity'.

'Camera One simply did what most cameramen would have done,' said Didier. 'He followed the action.'

'There's nothing worse than being left with a blank screen,' agreed the vision mixer. 'Besides, there was nowhere else to go. The other cameras had already peeled off. Two and Three were lining up reaction shots of the audience drinking champagne. Camera Four was in the middle of making a move.'

'So what happened after I left?'

'There was nothing anyone could do,' said Julian. 'My understanding is he was taken straight up to his apartment to await the arrival of the medics. As soon as his wife realised he was dead she asked to be left alone with him. We agreed of course.'

'She was in the audience?'

'No, she was watching the show from his apartment.'

Monsieur Pamplemousse tried a different tack. 'How about the Staff nurse?'

'The usual one was on holiday,' said Julian. 'She was from an agency. All she did was phone for help. I can get her name if you like.'

Before Monsieur Pamplemousse had time to reply the studio manager's voice broke in over the talkback. 'Ready when you are...'

'Right... stand by for a run through...' The director turned back to the desk.

'Sorry about this. Needs must. I wish you luck with finding out who did it, but not too much. And give whoever it was regards from us all.'

As though on cue, there was a burst of recorded applause from the sound gallery. It would have been music to Jacques' ears. So far he had yet to hear anyone with a good word to say about the deceased.

Pommes Frites was waiting for them behind the door when they got back to the apartment. He seemed excited about something. As soon as they entered he ran back to the kitchen.

'He looks as though he's trying to tell you something,' said Julian.

Monsieur Pamplemousse glanced at his watch. 'I think he is trying to tell me it is time for *déjeuner*. He is a stickler for punctuality.'

Stationing himself in front of a large store cupboard Pommes Frites braced himself and gave vent to his feelings in no uncertain terms.

The feeling of frustration had been building up inside him ever since he'd arrived in the apartment, so when the growl did emerge it was much louder than he had intended; louder and deeper, for it had travelled all the way up from the pit of his stomach, gathering momentum on the way. It made everybody jump, himself included.

'I wouldn't like to meet him on a dark night,' said Julian.

'Don't worry,' said Monsieur Pamplemousse. 'He wouldn't normally hurt a fly.'

'It's not the flies I'm worried about,' said Julian.

'People always associate Bloodhounds in their mind with the Hound of the Baskervilles,' said Monsieur Pamplemousse. 'But nothing could be further from the truth. They are the gentlest of creatures. Pommes Frites would only attack someone if he thought they were attacking me. It is their sense of smell they are most prized for. The holder of the record for the highest number of arrests is an American dog called "Nick Carter". He was responsible for over 600.

'Pommes Frites was sniffer dog of the year during his time with the Paris *Sûreté*,' he added proudly.

'On the other hand...' He recognised the signs. The set of the tail; the pulsating nostrils; the stiffening of the muscles... they were like a tightly coiled spring waiting to be released. '*Permettez-moi!*'

Flinging open the cupboard door, he stood back.

The middle shelf was like a miniature *épicerie*. Bottles and packets of various herbs, spices and other flavourings were neatly laid out in alphabetical order. Most of them looked unused. Without the slightest hesitation Pommes Frites homed in on the A's.

It was not what Monsieur Pamplemousse had expected.

'A good try though,' said Julian. 'How many arrests did you say he was he responsible for while he was with the police?'

'I didn't,' said Monsieur Pamplemousse gruffly.

'He took early retirement,' he added hastily, trying hard to hide his disappointment. Having given Pommes Frites such a large build-up it was galling to have him make the elementary mistake of confusing the smell of almond essence with that of cyanide. He felt let down.

The pager on Julian's mobile began to ring. 'Is there anything else I can help you with?' he asked.

Monsieur Pamplemousse shook his head. While he was waiting for the call to be taken he gave Pommes Frites a pat. Perhaps, like the rest of them, he was beginning to feel his age. It was all too easy to lose track of time.

'Randy wants to see you before you go,' said Julian.

'I should count your fingers afterwards if she shakes hands,' he added, as they parted company.

It sounded like good advice.

Chapter Seven

Ramona D. Katz was busy with the coffee machine when Monsieur Pamplemousse and Pommes Frites arrived back in her office.

'Ah, Mr. Grapefruit. You wanna cup?'

'Thank you, no.'

'Pity. It's arabica. I have it sent specially from *illycaffè* in Italy. It's the bees knees.'

'I'm trying to cut down,' said Monsieur Pamplemousse. 'Doctor's orders.'

'I like you, Grapefruit,' said Mademoiselle Katz. 'You have fine qualities. A straight talker like you should live to be a hundred and twenty. If things were different you and me could become an item.' She looked him straight in the eye. 'I'd hate anything should happen to you in the meantime.'

'Meaning?'

'Curiosity killed the cat. You want a piece of friendly advice? If I were you, for the time being I wouldn't walk under any ladders – it could bring you bad luck.' With her free hand she tapped the armband. 'I don't want I should have to wear another one of these. I have one too many already. Anyway, it's like I say... maybe we should meet up sometime. Your dog too. What's his name?'

'Pommes Frites.'

'Pommes Frites! I like it! We'd make a great *ménage à trois*.'

Monsieur Pamplemousse did his best to suppress a shudder at the thought.

'Sure you won't have a cup?'

'Certain.' The smell was out of this world. If he stayed much longer he might succumb.

'*Ciao*!' Madamoiselle Katz added four lumps of sugar to her cup. 'Give me a call if you change your mind. If you ever feel like an upgrade you know where to find me.'

'You shall be the first to know.'

He wondered. Death or dishonour? Becoming an item with the *Directeur Général* had all the makings of a fate worse than death. It was hard to picture what Doucette might say if they all arrived home together one evening.

There was a spring in Monsieur Pamplemousse's step as they left the *Centre de Télévision et Ciné de la Butte*. One way and another he wasn't sorry to be out and about in the real world again.

Pommes Frites hurried on ahead to investigate a man wielding an enormous pair of bolt-cutters. He was attempting to slice through a security chain on his parked motor-cycle. Or somebody else's motor-cycle!

Undoubtedly the latter, for as soon Monsieur Pamplemousse drew near he took one look and made off as fast as he could go.

Further down the Rue Lepic, towards Boulevard Clichy, a huge negro transvestite wearing a minuscule leopard-skin patterned dress slit up the side beckoned to them from a doorway as they went past, then just as quickly faded into the background.

It reminded Monsieur Pamplemousse of Mademoiselle Katz. Had she been issuing a genuine warning, or was it simply her idea of a joke? If that were the case it was in very poor taste. Not that taste probably figured largely in her repertoire. It was hard to picture what she went home to at night.

The world of make-believe took over once again as they neared the bottom of the Rue Lepic.

The *café-tabac* Les Deux Moulins, featured in the film *Amélie*, was packed to overflowing. Groups of tourists hovered outside, taking pictures of groups of tourists inside, taking pictures of them taking pictures. It was a form of perpetual motion.

According to Doucette the same scene was played out most days at a local greengrocers which had also featured in the film.

He seized the opportunity to complete the circle. It was a good chance to test the Director's latest investment. In his never-ending search for lightweight equipment, Monsieur Leclercq had acquired some Kyocera S5 digital still cameras. Thickness aside, they were of credit card dimensions; ideal for the unobtrusive recording of hotels and restaurants for *Le Guide's* archives.

Eye glued to the optical viewfinder rather than the small video screen – being a new toy he didn't want to risk putting too much strain on the battery – he concentrated on the task in hand.

It wasn't until he went to slip the camera back into his pocket that he realised Pommes Frites had disappeared. He was about to reach for the silent dog whistle he always carried with him, when he saw a familiar figure emerge from an *épicerie* on the other side of the road.

Pommes Frites bounded towards him, hotly pursued by a man in a white coat. 'Is this your dog, *Monsieur*?'

Having been singled out, Monsieur Pamplemousse could scarcely deny it.

'He should be on a leash! Can you not see the sign on the door? *Chiens interdit.*'

'He is a something of a gourmet,' said Monsieur Pamplemousse, doing his best to ignore the fact that Pommes Frites now had his eye on something remarkably obscene lying in the gutter. It looked like a chicken's

139

entrails.

'It is his day off,' he added, anxious to pour oil on troubled waters, 'but he never rests. He recognises true quality when he sees it.'

'Smells it you mean,' said the shop owner. 'It is bad enough when customers enter my shop and start nosing around, but dogs I can live without...'

Monsieur Pamplemousse followed the man back across the road. 'It comes naturally to a Bloodhound,' he said. 'They are born sniffers.'

'Through glass?' The shop owner pointed to a pile of jars on the floor. 'It took my girl half the morning to make them into a pyramid.'

Monsieur Pamplemousse had been about to offer to pay for any damage, but he changed his mind when he saw how many there were.

'He has an eye for labels too,' he said lamely. 'He may have been looking for something in particular.' A thought struck him as he took a closer look. 'Just lately he seems to have developed a taste for almonds...'

Pommes Frites didn't actually give vent to a sigh as Monsieur Pamplemousse selected one of the jars. Nor did he bother raising his eyebrows to high heaven when he saw him paying for it – they would have been scarcely visible amongst the folds in his skin if he had – but it was very frustrating. Clearly, for the time being at least, he and his master were on different wavelengths. It wasn't his fault the jar he was interested in had been in the bottom row. On closer inspection it hadn't been what he was looking for anyway.

'What about the others?' The man barred their way. 'They are covered in saliva. They will all need to be washed before they can be put back on display.'

Monsieur Pamplemousse braced himself. 'Doubtless

your girl – the one who made such an admirable job of stacking them in the first place, will be able to do it again in half the time now she is practised in the art.'

'Look here...' began the man belligerently. Monsieur Pamplemousse stared at him. 'No, you look here. Any more from you, *Monsieur*, and I will have your premises closed down for possession of drugs.'

'Drugs? I have no drugs...'

'You will by the time the boys have paid you a visit.'

'You wouldn't dare...'

'Try me!' said Monsieur Pamplemousse grimly.

It was a shot in the dark, but it went home. Ignoring the man's stammered apologies, Monsieur Pamplemousse led the way out of the shop. Once again, it was just like old times.

Following in his master's footsteps, Pommes Frites looked better pleased, as though he had got a point home at long last. His effort, too, had been a shot in the dark. Having drawn a blank, there was no point in wasting any further time on it.

Together they made their way down to the Boulevard de Clichy.

The sun was shining, and even the Place Blanche, not normally the most salubrious of sights during the hours of daylight, seemed to have an air about it. The freshly painted paddles of the mock windmill outside the Moulin Rouge, a symbol of Paris in general at the end of the nineteenth century and Montmartre's pastoral beginnings in particular, reflected the light as though they were proud of the fact and had every intention of keeping it that way.

The girls might no longer perform their dance routine inside a giant model elephant as they had done in the early days, but the windmill still turned slowly every night as though beckoning people to enter.

In many respects parallels could be drawn with Las Vegas. It was at night that the two really came alive. Las Vegas with its casinos; the Boulevard de Clichy with its massage parlours, sex shops, "live shows" catering for all tastes - *femmes, lesbiennes, couples, table danse*. Tattoo parlours, all-night cafés, hot-dog stands, clubs where the price of champagne rocketed skywards, the dazzling array of multicoloured neon lights; all played their part, merging into one vast montage given over to the pursuit of hedonistic pleasures.

And in the morning the police would send round the "salad basket" to pick up the flotsam and jetsam of human frailty, sending them on their way, richer or poorer for the experience.

While they were waiting for the traffic lights to change, the motorised Petit Train de Montmartre drew up alongside the central paved area. Monsieur Pamplemousse eyed the elderly passengers benevolently as they disembarked. They looked like members of an out-of-town *boules* club. He wondered what memories they would take back home with them.

As if in answer to his thoughts, a mixed group broke away from the main body and headed across the road towards *Pornissimo Ciné Sex*. They, at least, were playing it safe.

Those that were left would do well to hold on to their wallets, or to their female companion's apron strings. Most of the "girls" out to catch the lunchtime trade would look better after dark. Love might be for sale, but it was at a price. You got what you paid for, no more and often a lot less. Time was money. No one was admired for themselves alone and an old-age pension wouldn't go very far.

Setting off in an easterly direction towards Pigalle he passed a man holding forth to two others about a woman friend who had taken up the life of a pimp. Was there nothing sacred? She wasn't even including him in on the deal! As they squeezed past he stopped talking abruptly and stared after them.

Monsieur Pamplemousse returned his gaze.

The visit to the studios hadn't thrown up much in the way of new information. In retrospect he wasn't sure why he had gone there in the first place, except you had to start somewhere.

Jacques was right about one thing. If the powers that be were anxious to sweep the whole thing under the carpet, what was the point in him swimming against the tide? It was simply that old habits died hard and the whole thing was untidy. His appetite had been whetted. There was something about the affair that didn't quite gel.

In a sense, standing back and viewing things dispassionately from the sidelines, the question of who had killed Chavignol was of minor importance beside the finding of the photographs. It was more a matter of priorities, although he couldn't help feeling that solving one might provide an answer to the other.

In any case, with Chavignol gone they would still have Claudette to deal with, and in all probability she would show even less mercy than her husband when it came to the crunch.

A couple standing in the middle of the pavement were having a slanging match at the top of their voices.

Most of the passers-by gave them a wide berth, stepping into the road to get past. It was hard to tell what the row was about for it was more finger wagging and name-calling than anything. Monsieur Pamplemousse didn't fancy the man's chances. He was puny by the side of the woman. One swipe from her handbag would have floored him. Love made strange bedfellows.

Once again, as he squeezed past, close enough to be nearly asphyxiated by the smell of cheap perfume, they gave him a strange look and suddenly lowered their voices.

He wondered what it was about him that day. Did the fact that to all intents and purposes he was back on a case lend him a certain air? Once acquired, never lost.

The sight of the couple led to another thought. Both statistically and historically, poison was always thought of as being a woman's prerogative. He wondered how much of the story Claudette had told Monsieur Leclercq was true, or had she made it all up?

Had she been drawn in to Chavignol's world against her will, or had the boot been on the other foot? Experience had taught him not to be surprised by any aspect of human behaviour.

Whatever the answer, there were no two ways about it. The number one priority was to get hold of the photographs, and to do it as quickly as possible. Bungling the attempt would set alarm bells ringing and if that happened they might never be found. If his hunch that they were kept in Claudette's bedroom were correct – and apart from finding the safe, he really only had the Director's story to back that theory up – then with or without Jacques, help he must work out a plan.

While he was in the area, there was one other call he had in mind. Taking a turn to the left he set off up a side street.

Poupées Fantastiques was where it had always been; yet another monument to Montmartre's dedication to the pursuit of pleasure in all its forms.

Leaving Pommes Frites outside for the moment, he entered a tiny reception area, unchanged since his last visit.

The proprietor, Oscar, emerged from behind the scenes.

He, too, was as he remembered him; fat, oily, anxious to please; as unctuous in his way as Chavignol had been, but without his veneer.

'You may remember,' said Monsieur Pamplemousse by way of introduction, 'I bought a *gonflable* from you many years ago. It was an inflatable dog kennel, in fact. I had it specially made to my own design. It even had a place for the food bowl.'

'Monsieur Pamplemousse!' There was the familiar washing of the hands in invisible soap. 'I trust it gave you satisfaction.'

'It was not for me,' said Monsieur Pamplemousse stiffly.

Oscar gave him a wink. 'That is what they all say.'

Monsieur Pamplemousse stifled the reply he would have liked to make. It was hard to be cross with someone who remembered your name after the passage of so much time.

'You were a trendsetter, *Monsieur*. For a time we had a big run on kennels. With some it was a case of the smaller the better. Others, like you, went for broke, but then people grew tired of them. You perhaps wish to replace it? I have a few of the deluxe models left. They come complete with a battery-operated video camera and a packet of assorted condoms...'

Anxious to change the drift of the conversation, Monsieur Pamplemousse opened the shop door and called for Pommes Frites. There was barely room for the two of them.

Oscar took the point. 'My apologies, *Monsieur*.'

'How is trade?' asked Monsieur Pamplemousse.

Oscar gave a non-committal shrug.

'The death of Monsieur Chavignol hasn't affected you?' Again, it was a shot in the dark.

'Chavignol? The television chef?' Oscar eyed him cautiously. 'What made you ask that?'

'I know his tastes,' said Monsieur Pamplemousse. 'I know the kind of money he was prepared to spend. He would only go for the best.'

'Flattery will get you everywhere,' said Oscar. 'As for business, it is as it has always been – swings and roundabouts. You lose some ... you win some. Most of the time it is a matter of keeping one step ahead of the game. There is always a demand for something new. Since digital cameras came on the market nobody wants "private" film processing any more. They can watch everything on their own television screens as it happens. As for porno pics... it isn't so much what people are doing to each other these days, it's who's doing what to whom.

'Which reminds me. You were going to let me have some taken of you with those girls at the *Folies* – the ones that led to your being fired. How many girls was it? 'Twenty-five?'

'They were not *of* me,' said Monsieur Pamplemousse gruffly. 'They were supposedly taken by me. And the number is immaterial. It was a set-up. As for my being fired because of it – I took early retirement.

'Why am I here? It is because I am investigating Chavignol's murder. You would do well to co-operate. I would like to know how long you have had dealings with him? What kind of products you have been supplying him with? In short, anything and everything you can tell me about him. *Par exemple*, has he ever been into selling you pictures?'

'Not since the very beginning. In the early days, when he was still on tour, he used to send me photos from time to time. I think some of his assistants got more than they bargained for when they took the job. Folding themselves up when they were supposedly being sawn in two was the

146

least of their problems.'

He pointed to a poster on the wall showing a younger Claude Chavignol. Dressed in top hat and tails, he looked the archetypal magician.

'In the beginning he used to come in here occasionally. For minor items, you understand? Then, when he began to hit the high spots he switched to mail-order. As time went by he started looking for more exotic items ... that was when he opened an account. He's had one ever since.'

'So there would be records...'

'Records?' Oscar looked pained.

'What sort of things did he buy?' persisted Monsieur Pamplemousse.

'Come with me and I will show you...'

Leaving Pommes Frites to guard the reception area, Monsieur Pamplemousse followed Oscar into the back of his shop. It was like entering a waxworks museum.

'Inflatable nuns are the best-selling line, particularly those that come with, shall we say, rather more exotic optional extras than you might expect from someone who has recently taken the vow of chastity. Monsieur Chavignol favoured novices. I think perhaps he enjoyed picturing deflowering them before they had taken their finals. But he was not averse to the occasional Mother Superior.

'English Headmistresses come a close second. Articulated nurses are coming up fast.'

'Articulated nurses?' Oscar made it sound like a horse race.

'You can have them bending over while they are making the beds.' He led the way through some bead curtains. 'Monsieur Chavignol used to call this my Edith Cavell room. I don't know why.'

It could have been a field hospital at the time of the

Crimean War.

'They have to stand up to a lot of hard wear.' Oscar caught Monsieur Pamplemousse eyeing the selection of whips and scourges hanging from the walls.

'What used to be known as the English disease is becoming more and more popular. Word gets around. Only this morning I had a big order in from Marseille of all places. That is like sending *foie gras* to Gascony.'

'Nurse Cavell must be turning in her grave,' said Monsieur Pamplemousse drily. To have inspired Edith Piaf in the choice of a first name was one thing, but he doubted if she would appreciate having it coupled to Oscar's flights of fancy.

'She is someone you know?' asked Oscar, with an eye to business. 'You have her address?'

'Edith Cavell,' said Monsieur Pamplemousse, 'was an English nurse; a heroine of the First World War.' His wave embraced the whole of the display. 'Such things are hardly what she can have had in mind when she was appointed first matron of the Berkendael Institute in Brussels. While she was there she helped many wounded British, French and Belgian soldiers escape to the Netherlands. She ended up on October the 7th 1915 being shot by the Germans.'

'Such erudition,' said Oscar. 'There is no doubt, Monsieur P. you were a great loss to the Force when you took early retirement. It serves them right.'

Monsieur Pamplemousse decided it was time to go. There was nothing more to be gained.

On their way back to the Boulevard de Clichy, Pommes Frites received an offer he clearly had no difficulty in refusing, this time from a woman standing outside a massage parlour. It was one more than his master had scored. Things were coming to a pretty pass.

Having reached the Place Pigalle, Monsieur Pamplemousse mentally tossed a coin as whether or not to take the Montmartrobus home. There was one waiting at the terminus on the far side of the square.

Before he had a chance to reach a decision it moved off, so he decided instead to give Pommes Frites a treat, although in truth he didn't fancy doing it the hard way himself; there would be 250 or more steps to climb if they went on foot.

Turning into the Rue de Steinkerque he found himself trapped behind a swarm of Japanese tourists also making their way up the hill, taking pictures as they went. Their eyes were firmly fixed on a white flag attached to the end of a pole up ahead and there was no getting past.

Finally, he managed to overtake the party when they paused in the Place Saint Pierre. Cameras whirred and clicked as they took pictures of the ancient carousel.

Bypassing a quartet outside the entrance to the funicular, doing their best for Vivaldi as they struggled to rise above the sound of the fairground organ, he saw there was an empty cabin. Hastily boarding it, he staked a claim on a vacant seat at the rear. With luck he would be on his way before anyone else got on.

Like everything else it had gone "state-of-the-art". From being a twin track, counterbalance arrangement with one cab going up as the other one came down, it was now a funicular in name only, each car operating independently of the other. With automatic detectors controlling all the variables, such as the total weight of passengers, the journey time had been halved and the system was now able to carry up to 2000 passengers per hour, double the previous number.

The schoolboy in him was looking forward to the experience, and his heart sank when he saw the same white flag heading his way above the crowd surrounding the musicians.

Moments later his worst fears were realised. Cameras still clicking, the party of Japanese poured on.

Then, horror of horrors, the worst happened. Having automatically weighed the load and decided the full quota of passengers had been reached, a peremptory warning signal sounded and the doors of the cabin closed, leaving the tour leader stranded on the platform. He was fortunate not to have lost his pole. Cries of alarm went up from all around. It was as though an umbilical cord had been severed.

It struck Monsieur Pamplemousse that in a way it was symbolic. Parallels could be drawn with the *Centre de Télévision et Ciné de la Butte*. They, too, had lost their "tour leader"; their star performer, the man who had made it all possible. He hoped the company would survive. It was a highly professional undertaking – a city within a city – and he respected professionalism. It would be a pity to see it fall by the wayside. The great problem of course would be in keeping highly paid staff productive. If they weren't fully employed they would be on their way.

No sooner had they set off up the hill than his mobile rang.

'Two things,' said Jacques. 'The date for the funeral has been fixed...'

'Does that mean the autopsy has been completed?' Monsieur Pamplemousse tried to make himself heard above the hubbub.

'Death has been certified as being due to cyanide poisoning. The funeral is tomorrow at 14.30. Cimetière Montmartre.'

'So soon? That is not possible.'

'All things are possible,' said Jacques. He broke off.

'Where are you? Are you alright?'

'I am far from alright,' gasped Monsieur Pamplemousse.

The 40 second journey completed, he was caught on a tidal wave of anxious bodies as the doors opened and the passengers began making good their escape before anything more went wrong.

'You had me worried for a moment,' said Jacques when they made contact again. 'It sounded like sale time at Galeries Lafayette.'

'It was worse,' said Monsieur Pamplemousse with feeling. 'Much worse.' So much for Pommes Frites' treat, and his own come to that.

'Madame Chavignol has been pushing for it,' continued Jacques, 'and you know what that means. Surprise, surprise, the examining magistrate has agreed. He says that as there is no case to answer the funeral can go ahead.'

'Is it official yet?'

'No. They are trying to keep it as low-key as possible. Actually, between you and me, what he really said was: "Since we have no idea who did it and would rather not know, the sooner he is six feet under the better."

'Anyway, it means the house will be empty between say, 13.40 and – give or take a few minutes either way – say 15.30 to be on the safe side.'

'How about the staff?'

'The whole affair is by invitation only. The live-in ones – the chef and the manservant will be going. Any others are being giving the day off.'

'How do you know?'

'I asked one of them,' said Jacques simply.

'I've checked with Malfiltre. He is in town. I've told him to expect a call from you.'

'*Merci beaucoup,*' said Monsieur Pamplemousse drily. 'So

what is the second thing?'

'My information is that unless some distant relative turns up at the last minute and contests the will, everything apart from a Facel Vega car goes to Madame Chavignol.'

Monsieur Pamplemousse absorbed the various bits of news as he reached the Place de Tertre, by now awash with tourists. A Montmartrobus – he wasn't sure if it was the same one he had nearly caught – was forcing its way past, scattering the unwary right left and centre, much to their disgust. They looked as though they thought it had no right to be there at all. Jacques could have played his game for real.

'Can I ring you back?'

'I'm not going anywhere. Any developments your end?'

'I tell you one thing,' said Monsieur Pamplemousse, 'I have a feeling Pommes Frites knows something we don't. He is behaving very strangely.'

'So what's new?' said Jacques gloomily.

Happy to be back at last after a rather longer morning walk than he was used to, Pommes Frites hurried on ahead of his master and paused outside the apartment block in order to mark his arrival home in time-honoured fashion and at the same time register his territorial rights for the benefit of any other dogs who happened to pass that way.

It being a regular habit, he allowed his gaze to wander and, happening to glance skywards, noticed two men making their way along the topmost balcony. They seemed to be carrying a heavy load between them and even as he watched, they stopped at a point immediately above the entrance to the building and began lifting whatever it was onto the railings.

For a brief moment the three legs supporting Pommes

Frites' weight remained rooted to the ground; the pose was so fixed the whole ensemble might well have been mistaken for yet another bizarre work by Jean Marais, creator of Marcel Aymé's statue.

It was so striking, a passing tourist recorded the moment for posterity on his Instamatic, blissfully unaware as he went on his way that he was about to miss a photo opportunity that would have more than paid for his holiday.

Pommes Frites could have told him if he'd had the time. But he didn't. It dawned on him that if he were to stand the remotest chance of saving his master from almost certain death speed was of the essence. That being so, he sprang into action.

The dull thud as Monsieur Pamplemousse hit the paving had barely died away when a second crash echoed round the square, sending sparrows, pigeons and other lesser forms of wildlife fleeing in all directions.

Any satisfaction Pommes Frites might have gained from a mission accomplished was offset by the fact that in falling his master appeared to have knocked himself out.

He gave the bit nearest to him a tentative lick and having savoured the result, gazed down at it with interest.

Although his licks were widely recognised as being a panacea for a variety of ills, it was a long time since he'd had occasion to apply the treatment to his nearest and dearest. Such intimacies, whilst appreciated for the thought that lay behind them, were not normally encouraged on account of the wetness factor. That being so, he was surprised to discover the taste was not that of aftershave – which he didn't much care for, but that it bore a remarkable resemblance to a dish Madame Pamplemousse sometimes took out of her oven of an evening. You learnt something new every day.

It being one of his favourites he tried again, and this time something detached itself from his tongue, wakening his master in the process.

Monsieur Pamplemousse sat up. Slowly gathering his senses as everything around him swam back into focus, he was able to shed a little more light on the subject.

Removing a half-chewed object stuck to his cheek, he immediately identified it as a marjoram leaf, that classic accompaniment to roast lamb.

Worse still, only a few metres away, sprigs of what had once been healthy sorrel and fennel plants protruded from the shattered remains of a pottery *jardinière*.

The fact that he had narrowly escaped being killed was one thing; a matter he was to dwell on more fully in the days to come. To lose a sixth of his herb garden in one fell swoop was something else again.

Retrieving one of the broken stems, he eyed it gloomily. It was all that was left of his prize tarragon. Doubtless whoever was responsible for the outrage would be well clear of the building by now, but if he ever caught up with the person or persons unknown, he would personally make sure they would wish they had never been born.

Chapter Eight

'Doucette,' said Monsieur Pamplemousse, 'you must promise me never, ever to let anyone into our apartment again without finding out exactly who they are and why they want to come in.'

'But they seemed so nice, Aristide,' said Doucette. 'They told me they were from the *Mairie*. They had seen your picture in a *journal* and they wanted to inspect our balcony to make sure everything was safe.'

'Did they show you any form of identification?'

'They both had cards.'

'And of course you read them to make sure they were genuine?'

'Does anybody? It always seems so rude. Besides, I didn't have my reading glasses on.'

Monsieur Pamplemousse raised his eyes to high heaven. 'What did they look like?'

'They were both short and they had dark, pin-stripe suits. One of them looked a bit like that American film star – Edward G. Robinson. He was smoking a large cigar. I'm sure I would recognise them again if I saw them.'

'I can tell you one place you needn't bother looking,' said Monsieur Pamplemousse gruffly. 'That's anywhere within twenty kilometres of the *Mairie*.'

'They both had clipboards,' said Doucette defensively. 'It's what made it seem so official.'

Monsieur Pamplemousse sighed. 'Couscous, that is the oldest trick in the world. A clipboard is a symbol of authority. It will get you anywhere.'

'Anyway,' said Doucette, 'they didn't do any harm.

They were in and out in a matter of minutes.'

'I bet they were,' thought Monsieur Pamplemousse.

'The one with the cigar said what a nice apartment we had. He apologised for dropping ash on the carpet as he went out.'

She looked so contrite he didn't have the heart to pursue the subject any more. Besides, she had no idea what a narrow escape he'd had. If it wasn't for Pommes Frites' quick reactions... He shuddered; it didn't bear thinking about. It would be better not to tell Doucette. She wouldn't get any sleep if he did.

'I blame the media,' he said. 'I can't go anywhere at the moment without people recognising me.'

'Perhaps,' said Doucette, 'it is because you have your name written in large letters for all the world to see.'

Reaching out, she removed the studio's plastic name-tag from his jacket lapel and handed it to him. Monsieur Pamplemousse gazed at it sheepishly.

'What else have you been up to, Couscous?' he asked, resisting the temptation to add 'apart from putting out the welcome mat for two *loulous* who were clearly out to get me.' He hadn't exactly taken heed of Mademoiselle Katz's warning himself.

'I've been going through some old photographs.' Doucette pointed to an album lying half open on the dining-room table. 'Have you had a good day?'

'Have I had a good day?' It was hard to say. It was possible that somewhere amongst all the chaff there might be a few grains of wheat. He would need to sleep on it. In any case Doucette didn't wait for an answer.

'Do you remember this one you took of me on the Pont Neuf?' she said. 'It was just after you kissed me for the first time. On the back of the neck!'

'But you liked it!'

156

'I thought you were very forward. You had a moustache and it tickled. For a moment I thought it was a *mouche*.'

'In those days,' said Monsieur Pamplemousse, 'a moustache was considered to be a symbol of virility.'

'As I recall, Aristide,' said Doucette coyly, 'you had other ways of proving that. Shaving it off didn't seem to make a lot of difference.'

It wasn't until some years later that he had discovered Doucette classed men with moustaches as being in much the same category as those with beards; they were not to be trusted. The truth was more prosaic. At the time he had grown it more as a symbol of authority following early promotion. He had shaved it off straight away, of course, but it had been a salutary lesson in how two people could live together for years and still not reveal their innermost likes and dislikes to each other.

Doucette turned a page. 'Do you remember our first holiday in Nice? We stayed in a hotel near the flower market. You wouldn't go in the water because you said the pebbles hurt your feet.'

Monsieur Pamplemousse decided it was time to change the subject. He reached into his pocket. 'I have brought you a present, Couscous.'

'It isn't just for you,' he added, glancing down at Pommes Frites, who was hard at work removing the dust from his person following the encounter in the place.

'What a strange thing to buy,' said Doucette, taking the bottle from him. 'There are those amongst us,' said Monsieur Pamplemousse, 'mentioning no names, who seem to have got themselves hooked on the smell of almonds.'

'There are worse things,' said Doucette. She picked out another photograph. 'Remember when *you* smoked cigars?'

Monsieur Pamplemousse took himself into the kitchen before the conversation turned into a catalogue of his early imperfections. He returned a moment later with a small bottle of their own essence. Unscrewing the cap he placed it on the carpet.

Pommes Frites hardly bothered to look up from his ablutions.

'Perhaps he has gone off it,' said Doucette. 'You can have too much of a good thing. Besides, he looks as if he has more important things on his mind.'

'Talking of which...' Monsieur Pamplemousse glanced at his watch. 'I need to go out again. Pommes Frites can stay and look after you in case those men come back.'

Doucette knew better than to ask, but her normal *bonne journée* was tempered with a quizzical look as she saw him off at the door.

Pommes Frites looked even more worried, and he went out onto to the balcony to make sure the coast was clear, keeping watch until long after his master had disappeared from view along the Avenue Junot.

It was some while since Monsieur Pamplemousse had last seen Eddie Malfiltre and clearly life had been kind to him during the intervening years. Greying at the temples, casually dressed in immaculately pressed slacks and black polo-neck sweater, he could have passed for a business executive who had made his money and opted for early retirement. The tan hadn't come from a sun lamp, that was for sure, and when he moved he walked on the balls of his feet like an athlete.

Following a reasonably straight and narrow path obviously paid dividends. Knowing exactly where he stood, he didn't beat about the bush. Apart from there being no paperwork involved, Monsieur Pamplemousse might have been making arrangements to have an interior decorator pay a call or be seeking an accountant's advice on his pension arrangements.

'Jacques has given me the address and the time available.'

'Will it be enough?'

'What has been put together can be taken apart again. I have a map of the camp and I know what to look for, but it will need as much time as I can get. Rather more than I have been given if that is possible. If you could win me, say, another twenty minutes it would be a plus. You know what the 7th is like; crawling with flics on the look-out for anything unusual. I need to know exactly what you are looking for, and ideally where it might be located.'

Monsieur Pamplemousse filled him in on the former. There was no reaction.

'As for where you will find them... I strongly suspect they are in a safe hidden behind a picture of Chavignol in the main bedroom.'

'And you can guarantee there will be no one at home?'

'I am not in a position to guarantee anything,' said Monsieur Pamplemousse. 'But I will do the best I can, you have my word on that. It would not be in my interests to act otherwise. Give me your mobile number and I will let you know immediately if there are any changes.'

And that was it. Both sides had to take the other on trust.

On his way home Monsieur Pamplemousse phoned Jacques to tell him the meeting had taken place and it was all systems go.

'One thing, can you tell me which division of the cemetery is earmarked for the actual burial?'

Jacques consulted his file. 'The 17th... that's just inside the main gate. He'll be in good company, along with a lot of actors and writers. Why do you ask?'

'Because Malfiltre could do with more time. Somewhere further away from the entrance would be better.'

'In that case,' said Jacques, 'do you want the good news first or the bad?'

'Give me the bad,' said Monsieur Pamplemousse. 'It's nice being able to look forward to seeing light at the end of the tunnel.'

'Whoever said Chavignol is being buried was speaking figuratively. He's being cremated at Père Lachaise.'

'What!'

Monsieur Pamplemousse mulled it over for a moment. 'In that case we have more time than we thought.'

'Wrong. Père Lachaise happens to be the only place in Paris where you can be cremated. The ashes will be delivered to his wife immediately afterwards and she will take them on to Montmartre cemetery for the actual burial.'

'Why can't he be buried at Père Lachaise?' asked Monsieur Pamplemousse. 'It would make life a lot easier.'

'Because that's what everybody expects will happen. It was Chavignol's express wish that it should be a quiet affair.

'Dead men can't be choosers. He's lucky to get in anywhere at short notice. Someone must be pulling strings as it is. Death isn't the great leveller it once was. Space is at a premium and it costs. Since local councils lost their monopoly on the ownership of the land, cemeteries have become big business. I doubt if Montmartre is in quite the same league, but the last I heard Père Lachaise were charging Fr100,000 for a 15 year lease on a 2m square plot. If they took that route think what a burden it will be on Chavignol's nearest and dearest when the lease comes up for renewal.'

'That's a load of *conneries* and you know it,' said

Monsieur Pamplemousse. 'There's enough money there to buy a dozen plots. The whole thing stinks.'

'Am I saying it doesn't?' said Jacques. 'Why do you think I spend so much time knocking pedestrians down? If I didn't have my computer I might run amok and do it for real.'

'There must be something we can do to slow things up,' said Monsieur Pamplemousse. 'Are you sure you can't drop a hint to the press. That would bring in the crowds...'

'*Nyet, Nein, No...Impossible!*' said Jacques. 'When I say word has come down from on high, I do mean from on high. Life wouldn't be worth living if it got back that I had tipped the media off. They would be there like vultures with their cameras and their notebooks. Madame Chavignol is regarded as a loose cannon. There is no knowing how she will react if she is crossed. Short of phoning rent-a-crowd to foul up the proceedings, there is nothing I can do. I would if I could, but I can't.'

Monsieur Pamplemousse was listening with only half an ear, his mind going back over the day's events. Jacques' words had triggered off a thought. It was a wild one, but it might work.

'You couldn't rustle up fifty or so out of work Japanese actors could you?'

'It's funny you should say that,' replied Jacques. 'I have so many out of work Japanese actors on my books I don't know what to do with them. They're getting in my hair, which isn't easy as there's not much left...Look, I don't run a theatrical agency.'

'I am being serious.'

'Tell me why and I'll see what I can do.'

Monsieur Pamplemousse told him.

'Leave it to me.' Jacques suddenly perked up. 'I'll do better than that. I'll see if I can do something about the real thing. It's time the cemetery was on the tour circuit. Think of all the famous people buried there…Sacha Guitry, Emile Zola, Hector Berlioz, Francois Truffaut, Edgar Degas, Delibes, Offenbach, Nijinsky, Alexandre Dumas. Edmond and Jules de Goncourt, Stendhal…now Chavignol…'

Monsieur Pamplemousse cut him short. Jacques was a typical Aries; full of enthusiasms. He thought on his feet. In the old days they had worked well together. *Formidable* as some of their colleagues had it. But he needed to be kept in check.

'How about the *Centre de Télévision*?' he asked. 'Have they been warned to steer clear of the press?'

'They're as anxious as anyone not to rock the boat,' said Jacques. 'The last thing they want is to have Chavignol's death turned into a national day of mourning. It will only draw attention to their loss, so the less said about that the better as far as they are concerned.'

'There will be sunny spells today,' called Doucette as Monsieur Pamplemousse arrived home next morning with the *croissants*. 'That is if the sun is patient enough to wait until it can find a gap in the clouds.'

Monsieur Pamplemousse gave an answering grunt. Quite frankly, as long as the rain held off he didn't mind what the weather did.

'A man in Toulouse has murdered his wife after being happily married for over 29 years,' said Doucette. 'No one knows why.'

'Perhaps it was because she kept reading bits of the newspaper out to him when he had his mind on other things,' muttered Monsieur Pamplemousse.

'Speak up, Aristide,' called Doucette. 'I can't hear you.'

'Life is full of strange happenings,' said Monsieur

Pamplemousse. 'There is no accounting for some of them.'

Doucette looked up from her copy of the *Le Parisien* as he entered the kitchen. 'Aristide!' she exclaimed. 'Don't tell me you've been to the *boulangerie* looking like that. You haven't even bothered to shave. What must they have thought? As for that old suit ... you look like a *clochard!*'

'Good,' said Monsieur Pamplemousse. 'That, Coucous, is exactly how I want it to be.'

Doucette gave a sigh. 'I know there is no point in my asking, but I do hope whatever the problem is, it will soon be over.'

'I hope so too,' said Monsieur Pamplemousse fervently. 'For the moment, it is like today's sky, a grey area. We must hope the forecast is correct and the sun will eventually break through.'

It was shortly before 14.30 when Monsieur Pamplemousse and Pommes Frites found themselves a suitable vantage point on the narrow flight of steps leading down from the Rue Caulaincourt to join the tiny Avenue Rachel at a point just outside the entrance to the Cimetière Montmartre.

Initially, the fact that animals were forbidden entry had been a bit of a setback, but on second thoughts it struck Monsieur Pamplemousse that perhaps it was just as well. Apart from the fact that Pommes Frites was hard to disguise, the cemetery was a noted haven for stray cats, which wouldn't go down well. In any case, from where they were sitting he had a clear view of any traffic entering or leaving.

Impervious to looks of disapproval from others using the passage as a short cut, Monsieur Pamplemousse unfolded a car rug and spread it out – the steps were in almost permanent shadow and he had enough problems

163

as it was without getting piles. Placing his hat inside uppermost to mark the boundary of the rug, he carefully left room for Pommes Frites, set the Kyocera in readiness in case it was needed, and made himself comfortable.

They hadn't long to wait. At 14.55 exactly the funeral *cortège* arrived; a black Citroen, presumably carrying the remains of the deceased, followed by a second with the lone figure of Madame Chavignol.

Monsieur Pamplemousse reached for his camera. Despite everything, he couldn't help feeling touched when he zoomed in and saw her dabbing at her eyes with a handkerchief as the car went past.

A third car carried her servant, Yin, and another Asian he took to be the chef. Both looked suitably inscrutable. He swapped the camera for his mobile and dialled a number. It was answered almost immediately.

'She's arrived.'

While he was on the phone another car appeared; a large Renault, driven by Julian House. Next to him was the director of Chavignol's programme. The studio manager was visible through the back window; probably still in his combat trousers if the top half was anything to go by. There was no sign of Pascal, which was surprising, but as the car disappeared through the arch he glimpsed a shock of red hair rising above the rear window. He wandered what pearls of wisdom Mademoiselle Katz was throwing up on the subject of funerals, or was she for once holding her counsel?

He would dearly love to know what had caused her to issue her word of warning. Perhaps, fate having dealt her a whole handful of losing cards, she viewed everything else in life with the utmost suspicion. And who could blame her?

The thought so occupied his mind he nearly missed seeing a coach enter Avenue Rachel from the Boulevard de Clichy and head towards the entrance to the cemetery. It was followed by three more. They came to a halt just below him as the driver of the leading one found his way barred by a portable HALT sign that had been put back into place.

The man slid open his window and called to the gate-keeper, clearly asking for the sign to be removed.

Equally clearly the gatekeeper was having none of it. An argument broke out.

One by one, Tour Leaders climbed out of the other three coaches and began remonstrating, but the man was adamant. He pointed to a closely printed list of rules and regulations pasted up outside his office. There was enough reading matter to last the rest of the afternoon if that was the way they wanted to play it.

Faced with such an impossible task, those in charge bowed to the inevitable.

In a matter of moments the end of the street was full to overflowing as some two hundred or more passengers alighted and fanned into separate groups.

Flags held high they set off, first of all laying siege to the lodge just inside the gate in order to claim their free maps. Honour satisfied, they then headed off into the cemetery itself, reassembling almost immediately opposite the first gravestone on their right. Tour Leaders launched into their respective spiels on the family Guitry. Cameras clicked.

Having recorded the scene for posterity, Monsieur Pamplemousse pocketed his own camera. At this rate it would take them all the afternoon to do the Grand Tour. The chances of anyone making a prompt getaway from the cemetery were minimal.

Pushing their way through the crowd of tourists would be difficult enough. Getting past the parked coaches near to impossible, and backing the four of them out into the busy Boulevard de Clichy could take forever, particularly as the police were conspicuous by their absence. Malfiltre would have more than his twenty minutes worth.

Jacques had done him proud. Once he got the bit between his teeth there was no holding him. Monsieur Pamplemousse could picture the moment when he phoned the tour company; smooth but implacable.

'I know where you normally park is a designated area. Certainly you may continue parking there. There is nothing whatsoever to stop you. You will get a ticket, of course...

'I know there are signs up, but you shouldn't believe all you read...it is only for the one day...

'Now, for the sake of peace all round, I have a suggestion to make...'

It wouldn't surprise him to find Jacques had managed to persuade the Montmartre train to follow in the wake of the coaches as well. That would really set the seal on things; all those old age pensioners swarming everywhere in search of free kicks among the gravestones.

Monsieur Pamplemousse didn't wait to find out. Gathering his belongings, he made himself scarce. A few minutes later, ignoring the surprised glances of passers by, he climbed into his car which he had left parked on the central reservation of the Boulevard de Clichy, waited until Pommes Frites had settled himself in the passenger seat, then headed for home.

He had barely travelled a hundred metres when his phone rang. It was Malfiltre. The message was short and to the point.

'Complications. I think you should come. You will find me in a white van just around the corner from the house.'

Clearly, since he was avoiding specifics, Malfiltre wasn't

166

running the risk of being overheard; an admirable precaution in the circumstances. Monsieur Pamplemousse responded in like fashion.

'*D'accord.* I'm on my way.'

The van was where he had been told it would be; parked alongside an area of pavement where there was an open man-hole surrounded by a portable barrier.

Having first peered down the hole, Monsieur Pamplemousse tapped on the rear door of the van. A moment or two passed before it opened a crack.

Malfiltre's working clothes were considerably nattier than his own. Dark blue cotton overalls, soft soled shoes, baseball cap, and thin cotton gloves.

It occurred to Monsieur Pamplemousse that he was like an actor who was blessed with the sort of face that could play a thousand parts. Being able to submerge himself into the surroundings whatever they happened to be was part of Malfiltre's stock in trade.

He gazed around the inside of the van. There was hardly a square inch that wasn't covered by racks of equipment.

'Tell me the worst.'

'I drew a blank on the safe.'

Monsieur Pamplemousse's face fell. 'You are sure?'

Malfiltre looked pained. 'It is so full of jewellery there isn't room for anything else. So... I put plan B into action.

'As you probably know, the place is alive with video cameras. That being so, I substituted one of my own in the hope that I would be able to keep watch.

'Like the rest of them, it is movement operated, but unlike the others it isn't closed circuit. It can be switched on remotely when required, like so...'

Pointing to a small VDU above a console, Malfiltre pressed a button. A picture of Claudette's bedroom came

167

up on the screen. The camera must have been situated near the bathroom for it took in most of the wall opposite, along with the better part of the two beds.

Monsieur Pamplemousse couldn't help feeling that Oscar would have given a lot for such facilities in the V for *Voyeurisme* section of his shop.

'Anyway,' continued Malfiltre, 'I came back here to test it. It was lucky I did, because I nearly got copped!

'I had hardly settled down when it came on of its own accord. Someone else must have arrived home. Even more fortunate was the fact that I had taken the precaution of putting everything back to normal. Apart from the camera itself there is nothing to show anyone has been in. Unless whoever it is has any reason to look, I doubt if they will spot it.'

'Did you see who it was?'

Malfiltre shook his head. 'Not yet. The point is, the range of the transmitter is fairly minimal. If you want to make use of it I may have parking problems. If it arouses interest in the wrong quarters I could be for it...'

He left the rest to the imagination. Monsieur Pamplemousse could picture what would happen if anyone from the local *gendarmerie* saw what was inside the van. Given current security problems, putting two and two together and making five would be inevitable.

Reaching for his mobile he dialled Jacques' number. 'Can you talk?'

'Hold on a minute.' He heard the sound of a door being shut.

'Not good news.' Monsieur Pamplemousse gave him a brief run down on the situation.

'Leave it with me.' Jacques paused. 'By the way, while you are on, and totally nothing to do with what we've been talking about, but the analyst's report on the oyster shell has just landed on my desk. Guess what?'

Monsieur Pamplemousse wasn't in a guessing mood.

'There isn't a trace of cyanide. It is common or garden almond essence. Or rather, correction, common or garden is exactly what it isn't. The boys in forensic have really gone to town – that's why it took so long. It's a brand called Sainte Lucie, which isn't easy to come by. They drew a blank in Fauchon and Hediard, but struck gold in the *Grande épicerie* at Bon Marché in the 7th. *Arôme Amande Amère* it's called. 1.68 euros for 20 millilitres, no less.'

Switching off his mobile, Monsieur Pamplemousse bent down and patted Pommes Frites. It was no wonder he had been turning up his nose at all the other brands he had been trying. To think that he could ever have doubted his abilities! Seeing the look of affection on his master's face, Pommes Frites responded. His lick, warm, moist, and lingering said it all.

'Before you go,' said Malfiltre. 'There's something else you should know. I think Madame Chavignol is about to take off. You can't see it in the picture, but on the right-hand bed, just out of picture, there is a large suitcase...'

'When you say large...'

'It's no over-night bag, that's for sure. One of Louis Vuitton's biggest and best. It's expandable and comes with built in straps on the outside. It must be a special order because it has combination locks. I didn't have time to look inside because of them, but it weighs a ton.'

'Just the one case?'

'It's the only one that's out, but there are plenty more in a store-room leading off the bedroom. And leading off of that again – which I nearly missed – there's a room full of recording equipment linked to all the cameras. It's a regular little studio set-up; editing machines, digital print-out facilities for stills...'

'But no pictures as such?'

'None so far as I could see.'

Monsieur Pamplemousse asked for a print-out of the picture on the monitor, thanked Malfiltre for his help, and having promised to keep in touch, left him to it.

Quite why he chose to drive home the way he did – along the Rue de Grenelle, taking a right into the Avenue Bosquet and crossing the Seine via the Pont de l'Alma – he would never know. It wasn't the most direct route by a long way, but he felt in need of thinking time and thinking time would have been in short supply had he taken a more direct route through the centre of Paris. Or so he reasoned at the time.

It had been much the same in the old days. If ever he had been stuck with what seemed like an insoluble problem he had taken himself for a walk round the block; even the simplest change of scene could throw up a fresh slant on things and help put them in a new perspective.

Although he hadn't mentioned it to anyone, not even to Jacques, the attempt on his life bothered him more than he admitted. He wondered if there had been someone above Chavignol; someone else protecting their interests, perhaps even in league with Claudette.

Finding out the pictures weren't in the safe after all was little short of a disaster. He had been so sure that was where they would be. Too sure, as things had turned out. He toyed with the notion that Malfiltre, having seen what they contained, was holding out in the hope of cleaning up himself, then dismissed the idea. He had too much to lose to indulge in funny business like that.

If Claudette planned to leave town they would need to move fast. Stopping at some traffic lights he took a quick look at the print-out of the bedroom scene. There was something not quite right about it. For a start there was a silver framed picture on top of the unit between the two beds. It had caught his eye because he was almost sure it hadn't been there before. But there was something else different about the room...

The lights changed to green and he pocketed the picture.

As for the business with the oyster shell; that was something else to think about.

In the event, the contrast between his peaceful strolls along the Seine and the present route could hardly have been greater, and yet, once again, it was almost as though it had been meant, for if he hadn't taken it he would never have seen what he did see.

Coming off the bridge he found traffic in the vast Place de l'Alma had ground to a halt. It was the hour of *affluence*; cars and *autobuses* were nose to tail pointing in all directions. He had forgotten it was the third week in October when the Fashion Shows were in full swing. Barriers would be up in the Avenue Montaigne away to his right. Home to all the big names in the world of haute couture, it looked chock-a-block with traffic.

On the far side of the square, a police car came down the Avenue George V, its blue light flashing. Realising what was ahead of him, the driver did a quick U turn, turned on his siren, and hit the accelerator pedal. If they had been sent to sort out the traffic they'd clearly thought better of it.

Monsieur Pamplemousse looked in his rear view mirror. He had left it too late to do the same thing. The road behind him was jam-packed as far as the eye could see.

A Peugeot 207 ground to a halt alongside him and a little old lady got out. She began directing the traffic, leaving her husband at the wheel to cope as best he could with the situation.

Monsieur Pamplemousse reached for the Kyocera. It was a golden photographic opportunity; a classic Cartier-Bresson moment. It might even make the cover of *Le Guide's* staff magazine. If it did it would be his second this year.

Undoing two clips above the windscreen, he pushed back the canvas roll-top, climbed onto his seat in order to secure a better vantage point, zoomed out to the Kyocera's fullest extent, and seized the moment.

While he was at it he swivelled round in order to take a reverse angle shot of the scene and immediately froze.

He saw the car first. It was some three lanes away, but he could hardly fail to recognise the marque for it was twice as long as most of the other cars around. The radio was on, playing a current booming pop record, and the windows were wide open, almost as though the owner wanted to announce his good fortune to the world at large.

Zooming in, he added the 2X digital zoom extension for good measure. Strictly speaking it wasn't a zoom in the optical sense, but it effectively enlarged of the centre of the picture, which meant a loss of quality. All the same, even in the fading light, he managed to frame a decent close-up of the driver. He was hatless; hatless and bald. He also had a moustache. It had to be Pascal. Jumping the gun by the look of it, probably on the basis that possession was nine tenths of the law. Claudette was probably glad to get rid of such a car, but it would serve both of them right if someone else came along – a long forgotten relative – and contested the will.

Monsieur Pamplemousse toyed briefly with the idea of leaving Pommes Frites in charge of his own car for the moment, in the hope of having a quick word, but without warning, almost as though a cork had been pulled from a bottle, the traffic began to move.

As he slid back down into the driving seat, he heard the full-throated roar of a 630bhp Police-tuned engine rising above the noise of the other traffic and he was just in time to see the driver accelerating away as to the manner born. Seconds later the Vega's tail-lights disappeared from view in the general flow of traffic.

Putting his own car into gear, he found himself wondering why, if Pascal was that mobile, he hadn't been at the funeral. It was possible, of course, that he hadn't been invited, but that seemed unlikely after such a long and close association. He would have to check on that. Maybe he had something to hide, or he didn't want to be seen by Madame Chavignol? Or *with* her?

Perhaps the simple explanation was that he had been worried about arriving at the cemetery only to suffer the indignity of finding the doors on his new car wouldn't open? Perhaps. And then again, perhaps not.

'Well?' said Doucette when he arrived back. 'I hope you got what you wanted.'

'During the time we were at the cemetery,' said Monsieur Pamplemousse, 'I made half a euro, three English pennies and two American coins of some kind.

'Pommes Frites did even better. He was given the remains of a hamburger and some popcorn. Oh, and we had our photograph taken by the American who left the coins. I don't think he had ever seen a *clochard* using a mobile telephone before.'

He could have said a lot more, but he wasn't sure where to start.

Chapter Nine

'*Merde*!' Monsieur Pamplemousse sat up in bed with a start. Groping for the light switch, he felt Doucette turn to face the other way.

'Must you, Aristide?' she groaned. 'What time is it?'

Screwing up his eyes he peered at the digital clock until the green bits came into sharp focus. '03.23.25.'

'But that's nearly half-past three in the morning,' said Doucette, after she'd had time to think it through.

'It's even worse now,' grunted Monsieur Pamplemousse. 'It's 03.24.07.' He lay back on his pillow. 'I was in the middle of a dream.'

'Whatever it was about,' said Doucette, turning round to face him, 'you seemed to be doing a lot of dithering. First you were shouting "*Oui, oui, oui*," the next moment it was "*Non, non, non*". I thought you were going to fall out of bed at one point you were struggling so.'

'I think you must have miscounted, Couscous,' said Monsieur Pamplemousse virtuously. 'I am sure there were more "*nons*" than "*ouis*".'

'I know what I heard,' said Doucette. 'It sounded more like groans of pleasure. *And*,' she added, 'your pyjama jacket is half off.'

Monsieur Pamplemousse sat up again and began struggling to find a spare opening for his left arm. There seemed to be rather more options than he remembered there being when he went to bed.

'I think,' he said, 'you will find it is half on. There is a big difference between the two, you know, Doucette. I have told you that before. It is like saying a bottle of wine is half empty when it would be equally true to say it is half full. The implications are very different.'

'That,' said Doucette, 'depends on whether or not you feel guilty.'

Monsieur Pamplemousse was tempted to say she hadn't been in his dream, but he decided discretion was the better part of valour. It was not the moment for scoring points.

Neither was it all that easy to explain, for it had been more than just a dream. In much the same way that he found a change of scene could be conducive towards solving a problem, so it was with sleep. Instead of letting his subconscious remain idle, metaphorically gathering dust as it were, he was a great believer in having that part of his mind do some of the donkeywork for him while he was in the arms of Morpheus. The brain was a wonderful piece of machinery. Feed it with a number of disparate thoughts and ideas in the few moments before dropping off and it was amazing what it could come up with by the morning. In the past some of his most successful cases had been solved that way. It was like taking advantage of cheap rates on the telephone.

On the other hand, such ploys did have their down side. While it was working away on its own, concentrating on sorting out random bytes of information under cover of darkness, the brain rarely had time for such niceties as the conversion of reveries into the equivalent of a three-dimensional Technicolor movie with stereoscopic sound.

Going to sleep hoping to dream about something, or indeed someone in particular, rarely bore fruit. In his experience that was especially so if the thoughts happened to be of an erotic nature. When that was the case, they often involved the most unlikely people. He'd once had a particularly vivid dream involving his sister-in-law and a large piece of tripe. He had never told Doucette, of course, and anyway it hardly came under the heading of being erotic; more of a nightmare brought on by a bad attack of indigestion following one of her meals. All the same, it had taught him never again to have a second helping out of politeness!

Occasionally, though, there were exceptions to the rule, and his fantasy involving Claudette Chavignol was a prime example. He would have been the first to admit she had been on his mind when he retired to bed that night. The picture of her *boudoir* on Malfiltre's monitor was vividly etched on his mind, and inevitably his thoughts had turned to their earlier encounter. Recalling the moment, he could still hear the rustle of silk, the sound of tearing fabric, the feel of the thick pile carpet beneath his feet, followed by the warmth of her urgent flesh against his as they collapsed into a heap on the floor, weighed down more by circumstances outside his control in the shape of Pommes Frites than from any pangs of conscience.

Much as he loved his friend and mentor, there were times when he wished he wasn't quite so quick off the mark. There was no doubting that he meant well, but his enthusiasm occasionally got the better of him. In retrospect, leaving a couple of beats before putting in an appearance that afternoon wouldn't have come amiss.

As he allowed himself to be embraced once more by the god of sleep, Monsieur Pamplemousse was filled with remorse. Pommes Frites was the best, the most loyal of companions. Had he not reacted with speed and accuracy outside their apartment only a day and a half ago, dreams of any kind might have been forfeited for ever.

In the beginning, apart from the running order being in reverse, his fantasy had more or less manifested itself in a repeat performance of the real thing. The main difference was that he had been in Claudette's *boudoir* to start with – for some reason wearing a pair of pyjamas that had seen better days – and it was she who had entered the room, clad only in the briefest of diaphanous black silk *negligées*.

He had been caught red-handed trying to open her suit-case with a nail file. And it was that, more than anything else, that caused the rot to set in. From then on it had been downhill all the way; or uphill, depending on where you happened to be standing.

There had been a quality of inevitability about the whole thing. To be sure there had been the same familiar moments – another case of "something old, something new"; the same rustle of silk as Claudette slipped out of her garment, the very same luxurious feel of the carpet beneath his feet. Only the sound was different; a shivering glissade from the harps as her *negligée* fell to the floor, followed by heavenly music welling up from the full orchestra as she ran towards him, arms outstretched: André Kostelanetz's interpretation of "Moon Love" rather than the Blue Danube sprang to mind.

It was when she realised what he was up to that she suddenly changed character.

Steam didn't exactly issue from her nostrils, nor did she paw the ground, like a bull about to give chase having scented blood. But her nipples, never slow in coming forward during moments of stress, as he remembered only too well, seemed to grow into battering rams before his very eyes, reminding him irresistibly of Jane Fonda in *Barbarella*.

Not only had he nearly ruptured himself when he went to lift the case off the bed, but as he tried to run off with it, his feet had turned to lead.

By then she was on him. Biting, scratching, clawing; her

tongue probing, searching for pastures new; her pelvic thrusts reminiscent of a pneumatic drill going full blast.

In retrospect, with only a small nail file to protect himself, that must have been the moment when Doucette heard his *ouis* turn to *nons*, for it was really quite painful and he had begun to fear for his life as she forced him backwards onto the bed.

That was something else he couldn't possibly explain to Doucette. She would immediately want to know how it was that he had dreamt of Claudette's bedroom if he had never been in it before. Women had a tendency to get diverted by such minor details and in so doing lose sight of the whole point of a story.

All he remembered as came up for air was having a brief glimpse in close-up of the picture in its silver frame; and there, in his dream, he had struck gold. The first time he'd seen it had been on the dressing table in Chavignol's apartment at the studio.

It was then, just at the *moment critique*, when both music and emotions were reaching a crescendo, that the door burst open and Pommes Frites rushed in, tongue hanging out and all systems at go. It was very much like the arrival of the cavalry in an old-time Western movie, but without the benefit of their bugles.

Coming to with a start, he realised Doucette was still talking to him.

'You've got your trousers off as well!' she said accusingly. 'Are you sure you are all right?' Placing a hand on his forehead, she then compared it with her own. 'It feels as though you have a temperature. Perhaps I ought to telephone the doctor?'

'I think a cold shower might be more efficacious,' said Monsieur Pamplemousse. After such a dream it was no wonder he had woken up covered in perspiration.

'In October?' Reaching forward to help him with his pyjamas, Doucette gave a start.

'Aristide!' she exclaimed. 'What *have* you done to your back? It's covered in scratches...'

Monsieur Pamplemousse's heart sank. It was fatal to lower your guard for a second. Having spent time judiciously practising some difficult sideways manoeuvres before climbing into bed, movements he had honed to perfection in front of the bathroom mirror, he could have kicked himself.

'I think they must be old ones, Couscous,' he said lamely.

'*Old* ones?' repeated Doucette. 'They don't look very old to me. They are still bright red!'

'Relatively speaking, of course...'

'Relative to what?' demanded Doucette. 'Or to *whom*?'

Seeking refuge in the light switch, Monsieur Pamplemousse gave up the struggle and lay back.

'Just relative,' he murmured, adding a gentle snore for good measure.

Luckily there was no need to keep up the pretence for more than a moment or so. Doucette invariably went straight back to sleep as soon as her head touched the pillow, and much to his relief that night was no exception. He had other pressing matters on his mind.

Although he still couldn't put his finger on it, as with the image on Malfiltre's screen, so it had been in his dream. Apart from the silver picture frame, which had contained a photograph of Chavignol's assistant, Pascal – without his hat as bald as a coot, there was something else not quite right about Claudette's *boudoir*. Another detail that kept eluding him. An ornament not in the right place, perhaps, or something missing...

In the no-man's land halfway between being awake and

falling asleep the answer came to him and the realisation set his mind racing.

'*Sacré bleu!*'

Doucette groaned as the light came on again. 'What is it now, Aristide?'

'Tell me something, Couscous,' said Monsieur Pamplemousse. 'Where does a wise man hide a pebble?'

'Must you start asking riddles at this time in the morning?' demanded Doucette.

'You *should* know the answer,' said Monsieur Pamplemousse. 'It was you who gave me the clue in the first place... showing me those old photographs.'

'You mean the ones taken in Nice? I suppose the answer is where there are a lot of other pebbles – like the beach near where we were staying. If you remember I found one shaped just like a cat, then I put it down for safe keeping and we never found it again.'

'*Exactement!*'

That was it. The parallel had been staring him the face all along. Where was the simplest to place to hide a photograph? In an album of course! And what was different about Claudette's bedroom as seen on Malfiltre's screen? The shelf in the glass-fronted cabinet between the two beds had been empty. The books were missing. Except, of course, he would be willing to bet they hadn't been books as such! He could have kicked himself for not having thought of it sooner.

If that theory were correct, the most likely answer to their present whereabouts, given its weight, was inside the suitcase.

And if Claudette was about to set off for goodness knows where taking the case with her, they would have to move quickly. To lose track of her at this stage would be like letting go of a cannon at the top of a steep hill and watching it gather speed. Who knew where it would end up, and at what cost on the way?

'*Now* where are you off to?' asked Doucette sleepily, as he reached for his dressing gown.

'I have a telephone call to make, Couscous.... I shan't be long.'

'At 03.40 in the morning?'

He looked at the clock. '03.42.'

'There are times,' said Doucette, burying her head under the duvet, 'when I wish I had never married a Capricorn!'

Much to his surprise, Jacques picked up his call on the second ring.

'What kept you?' asked Monsieur Pamplemousse.

'It took me that long to get dressed and rush downstairs,' said Jacques. 'I'll tell you something else for free. Half the household is not amused. And that's just me. The other half is livid. Yours is the second call I've had since we went to bed. I tell my wife; if she values her sleep so much she shouldn't have married a policeman. What's the problem? It had better be good.'

Jacques listened while Monsieur Pamplemousse told him.

'That's pretty good,' he said. 'Not perfect, but will do for the time being. Now, since you are on the blower I have news for you. I haven't exactly been idle.

'Claudette Chavignol is booked on Friday's 12.35 Air France flight from Charles de Gaulle to Marseille. I even have her seat number – it's 1A in the business section, so she should be among the first off the plane when it arrives...'

'Are you sure?'

'As sure as I am that it's a quarter to four in the morning. And how do I know that? Because my wife has just reminded me of the fact. I would have but I didn't want to disturb you.'

Monsieur Pamplemousse ignored the last bit. The word Marseille rang a faint bell in the back of his head.

'Friday!' he repeated. 'But that's today...'

'Sometimes,' said Jacques, 'I don't know how we've managed to survive all this time without your incisive mind at our disposal. I suppose the truth is they couldn't find two people to replace you, so they got computers instead.

'The point is... do you think she'll have everything with her? Prints, negatives and all?'

'I'm sure she will,' said Monsieur Pamplemousse. 'It doesn't sound as though she's going away for the weekend, and I can't picture her being one of the world's great readers. If she's doing a flit she won't want to risk being parted from them any longer than she has to. They're much too precious.'

'Fancy a trip to Marseille?' asked Jacques. 'City of probity, rectitude and seafood restaurants? I can fix it so that you catch an earlier flight. There's one at 10.40. That'll give you plenty of time to work out the lay of the land before meeting her plane and seeing where she goes. It should be just up your street.'

'I would need to clear it with my Director first...' said Monsieur Pamplemousse dubiously.

Jacques' mind was running on ahead of him as usual. The more Monsieur Pamplemousse thought about it the less the idea appealed to him. For a start he wouldn't be able to take Pommes Frites on the plane.

'Think *bouillabaisse*,' said Jacques.

'At this time in the morning?'

'Well, for the time being, think restaurants. Think smells... the sea... the Miramar restaurant in the old port...

Then think *bouillabaisse...*'

'It won't work,' said Monsieur Pamplemousse. 'She's almost bound to catch sight of me at some point, then the cat really will be out of the bag.' Realising he hadn't let on to Jacques the depth of his own involvement with Claudette, he wondered whether he ought to or not.

Deciding it was too early in the morning for confessions, he tried another tack.

'In any case, I have no power. Suppose Marseille is only a stopping off point. Just suppose she moves on. She could take a plane or a boat to practically anywhere in the world.'

'Anything is possible,' admitted Jacques. 'But if that's the case, why go there in the first place? I tell you something else the computer has thrown up. Guess when the booking was made?'

Monsieur Pamplemousse had no idea. He was beginning to lose all sense of time. He made a wild guess. 'Yesterday?'

'Three weeks ago...'

'Three weeks... *Morbleu!*'

'Exactly my sentiments. Look, if you don't fancy being on your own I could probably arrange help at the other end, but that would take a bit of explaining. The less people involved the better. I might even go myself. I could do with a spot of fresh air. Do you want a short list of all the possibilities, or a long one...'

'Apart from anything else,' broke in Monsieur Pamplemousse, 'there has already been one attempt on my life...'

'Seriously?'

'Seriously. Either that or a warning shot that was too close for comfort.'

'Sapristi! When?'

Monsieur Pamplemousse told him.

'But who would want to do that?'

'Quite a few people over the years, I imagine. But in this particular instance it must be someone who feels I may be getting close to the truth. Not only that, but someone who has killed once and wouldn't hesitate to do it again.'

'Or with sufficient clout to have someone do it for him,' added Jacques.

'Going back to the problem in hand,' said Monsieur Pamplemousse. 'We must stop Madame Chavignol leaving Paris at all costs.'

'Maybe we could pull her in at the airport?' Jacques tried another tack. 'We could get Security to go through her bags.'

'Would that be wise?'

'Just clutching at straws. You're right, though. Once those boys get their hands on the pictures who knows where they might end up? On their canteen wall most likely! It could defeat its own object.'

'Anyway,' said Monsieur Pamplemousse, 'they won't be in her hand luggage. If my hunch is right they'll be in the baggage hold of the plane.'

'Bags can go missing,' mused Jacques. 'It happens all the time. It's one of those things people take for granted. They only grumble when their own case gets lost. Have you ever been behind the scenes at Charles de Gaulle? It's like watching one of those giant machines the P.T.T. use for sorting mail, except it's spread over a much bigger area. The wonder is not so much that things go astray; it's the fact that it doesn't happen more often.'

'There's one big snag,' said Monsieur Pamplemousse. 'Hers won't be the only item of Louis Vuitton luggage heading for the South of France. You can bet your life on that. Identifying the right one and getting it out of the airport without doing a lot of explaining would be something else again.'

While Jacques was talking his mind had been racing on ahead. 'I have an even better idea.' He borrowed a leaf out of the Director's book. 'Perhaps I could run it up the flagpole and see what you think.'

It was also a case of role reversal. He was now the one thinking on his feet, and give him his due, Jacques was proving a good listener.

'I can't see any reason why it shouldn't work,' he said at last. 'We shall need to play it carefully and not tread on too many toes. It'll be a question of territories.

'We shall need a couple of extra bodies, but that shouldn't be a problem. There are so many identity checks these days, what's one more?'

'I can look after the check-in side of things,' said Monsieur Pamplemousse. 'That will save one. I'm afraid the rest will be up to you.'

'Leave it with me,' said Jacques. It was fast becoming his signing off phrase.

'See you at Charles de Gaulle airport. Outside Terminal 2D. The flight leaves from gate 70, so it will be somewhere near the Paris end of the terminal. Better make it eleven fifteen to be on the safe side.'

'I'll be there.'

'Don't forget to bring Pommes Frites.'

'As if I would!' said Monsieur Pamplemousse.

'And drive carefully!'

Monsieur Pamplemousse had two calls to make in the 7th before joining the *Périphérique* and then the A1 to Charles de Gaulle. Despite the delay he still reached the airport first.

Jacques looked slightly put out. 'If this place gets any bigger there won't be much point in taking a plane,' he complained. 'It will simply be a case of calling in for a refuel and a cup of coffee, then driving where you want to go. 3000 hectares. That's a third the size of Paris!'

As they entered the vast Departures hall he took one look at the people milling around. 'It could end up being quicker too.'

Taking advantage of a relatively quiet spot behind a magazine store, he produced a selection of clip-on identity tags. Monsieur Pamplemousse recognised the photo on his as having recently appeared in one of the *journaux*. Jacques must have moved fast.

'You are now a temporary member of Special Services Group – Section F. It will get you most places you need to go, but not necessarily all. If anyone asks what you are doing give them a good earful. Tell them you are not at liberty to say.'

'Do the *Sûreté* know about it?'

Jacques sighed. 'Questions, questions! Let's just say those who matter do. Look, as I've said before, there are so many checks going on at the moment they are beginning to be taken for granted. Just don't put it on your CV.'

'What CV?' said Monsieur Pamplemousse. 'They didn't have such things in my day.'

He slipped the tag into his pocket. There was no point in attracting attention unless it became absolutely necessary. In his experience "those who mattered" would probably deny all knowledge of him if it came to the crunch.

'I've got one for "you know who" as well,' said Jacques. 'Just to be on the safe side. Do you think he'll mind?'

Monsieur Pamplemousse glanced at the photograph as he attached it to Pommes Frites' collar. 'He ought to be pleased. He's aged a bit since this was taken.'

'You're sure he won't have forgotten what he's supposed to be looking for?'

'Now you *are* likely to offend him,' said Monsieur Pamplemousse. 'Besides, I gave him a little reminder on the way.'

He glanced up at the nearest bank of monitors. Most of the flights, including the 12.35 AF7674 to Marseille, were scheduled to leave on time.

Jacques led the way up a flight of stairs to their left where a balcony outside the Club Class lounge afforded an overhead view of the whole of the check-in area. It could have been purpose built.

The check-in section itself was momentarily empty, which was more than could be said for Economy. There were long queues at all the desks.

Monsieur Pamplemousse wondered what his old mother would have made of it all. He could hear her voice: "I can't think where they're all going." But then she had never been up in an aeroplane, or travelled outside the Auvergne, let alone seen the sea.

While they were waiting they went through the plan once more.

No one entering or leaving the lounge seemed surprised by the presence of two men with a large Bloodhound. The few who happened to glance their way looked reassured rather than apprehensive. It was a sign of the times.

At 11.52 Madame Chavignol appeared, immaculate as ever. Figures wandering aimlessly about the hall gave way automatically as she headed towards the check-in area.

Monsieur Pamplemousse nodded in her direction. 'She's here. Steel grey tailored suit, low heeled travelling shoes. You can't miss her.'

'Not exactly deep mourning,' murmured Jacques, unconsciously echoing Monsieur Pamplemousse's own

188

thoughts when he had first met Claudette.

A man pushing a trolley piled high with luggage followed her. 'Who's that?'

Monsieur Pamplemousse reached for his camera.
'Chavignol's ex-gofer, man-of-all-work, general factotum,
faithful retainer...'

'Are you sure about the faithful bit?' said Jacques, as
they passed below them. 'I don't think much of his suit,
but if the Hermès tie is anything to go by it looks as
though he could be on to a good thing. Do you think he's
travelling too?'

Monsieur Pamplemousse shrugged. 'Who knows? As
for the tie, it goes with the job.'

He realised it was the first time he had seen Pascal in his
entirety. He was taller than he had pictured; but then
Chavignol had been too, which figured. It was not dissim-
ilar to two people entering into a relationship having
spent the first few days gazing at each other full-face from
across a succession of restaurant tables; sometimes the
wider view, or an unexpected expression caught when
they weren't looking could prove a bit of a let down. By
then, it was often too late.

So it was with Pascal. In contrast to his ex-boss he
looked down-at-heel; seedy. It was amazing the difference
a good tailor could make.

Was he going too? The same thought had gone through
his own mind more than once since he'd heard how long
ago the flight had been booked.

He gave Jacques a nudge.

A little further down the hall another trolley had
appeared from out of nowhere. If anything, it looked even
more heavily laden than Pascal's. So much so, whoever
was in charge seemed to be having difficulty maintaining
a straight line.

'It looks like an unguided missile of the very worst kind,' said Jacques.

The two trolleys began closing in on each other, both apparently oblivious to the other's presence. Seen from above, short of one or the other taking last minute evasive action, the outcome was a foregone conclusion; an accident in the making. Luckily no one down below seemed to notice or take it upon themselves to interfere.

It was all over in a matter of seconds. Both parties recovered and went on their way.

Monsieur Pamplemousse breathed a sigh of relief. During the brief exchange of words following the collision he had taken a quick snap of the scene. The Director's camera was proving invaluable. Besides, Malfiltre might like one for the record.

'The man pushing the second trolley looked familiar,' said Jacques thoughtfully as it disappeared.

'Did he now?' said Monsieur Pamplemousse. 'It's a small world.' He watched as Claudette and Pascal reached the check-in desk.

'Mission accomplished?' asked Jacques.

'Pommes Frites will let you know in a little while.'

Hearing his name Pommes Frites made as though to get up, but at a signal from his master he remained where he was.

'Will it be a walk-on gate, or one where they get bussed out to the plane?' Monsieur Pamplemousse watched Claudette hand her ticket in at the desk.

'It's all taken care of,' said Jacques. 'It's buses. The further away from the terminal building they are the better.'

'Pity about the case. Malfiltre reckoned it's one of Louis Vuitton's best and he should know.'

'You always did have a sentimental streak,' said Jacques.

'I hate waste.' Monsieur Pamplemousse waited until Claudette had completed her registration. Clearly Pascal wasn't travelling with her. On the other hand, their perfunctory goodbyes after a brief chat left him with the feeling that it was only a matter of "watch this space" before they next met up.

He glanced at his watch. 'We ought to be on our way too. It would be a shame to miss the flight.'

Chapter Ten

'An elegant solution, Aristide,' said Monsieur Leclercq. 'I must congratulate you.'

'It had a lot to recommend it,' said Monsieur Pamplemousse modestly, 'but I couldn't have done it alone. I had help from an old colleague, along with someone who was once in the *milieu*, and Pommes Frites of course. In effect it was an arm's length transaction. Once everything was in position all the dirty work was done for us.'

'I cannot wait to touch base with you,' continued the Director. 'But never forget, the first aim of *Le Guide* is to report on food. *Michelin*, originally given away free when it first came out in 1900, was ostensibly published for the benefit of motorists, although in fact its underlying aim at a time when there were only 3000 registered cars in the whole of France, was to get people to become more motor minded so that in turn they, *Michelin*, would sell more tyres.'

Monsieur Pamplemousse stared across the dining room table at his boss.

He was used to the sudden flights of fancy; the unforeseen excursions into uncharted waters. Indeed, there were times when it was hard to keep pace with them. But seeing he had travelled all the way to Monsieur Leclercq's country home some thirty kilometres outside Paris for the express purpose of bringing him up to date on the current crisis over the photographs, it seemed a bit of a non-sequitur.

His host had also begun pulling strange faces, screwing

up his eyes as though in pain, and for a brief moment Monsieur Pamplemousse wondered if he had suffered a minor stroke brought on by the excitement of the occasion. With that possibility in mind he decided to humour him.

'I have always understood that was especially true following the introduction of the pneumatic tyre,' he said. 'In their early editions *Michelin* placed more emphasis on garages than they did on restaurants.'

Monsieur Leclercq visibly relaxed. 'That is why our founder, Monsieur Hippolyte Duval, stuck to his *bicyclette*. His theory was that people who used such a basic method of propulsion arrived at their destination far hungrier than those who travelled by train or car, and therefore appreciated a good meal all the more. For many years he refused to give up hard tyres as a matter of principle. In those days, of course, bicycle tires were glued to the rim anyway, but he viewed the arrival of pneumatic tyres with the utmost suspicion, believing it was a sign that France was going soft physically as well as spiritually.

'Times change; even the two hour break for *dejeuner* is no longer sacrosanct.'

Monsieur Pamplemousse's heart sank. He hoped the Director's last remark didn't mean their own lunch was going to be cut short. He had already told Doucette he wouldn't be wanting any dinner.

He relaxed as an elderly lady wearing a white overall and a chef's toque materialised alongside him bearing a plate of *risotto*. He hadn't even realised she was in the room. It was no wonder the Director had changed the subject so abruptly.

His spirits rose still further when she produced an ancient grater and began adding shavings of white truffle across the top of the rice. The smell of truffles mingling with that of the cheese was heaven sent.

'Parmigiano-reggiano,' said the Director of the latter, 'cut from the wheel. Maria refuses to buy so-called Parmesan that has already been grated. It is the same with the rice. Her choice is *vialone nano*. Nothing else will do.

'Please go ahead. It is one of her specialities – what our American friends would call her "signature dish". She will be most upset if you allow it to spoil. Is that not so, Maria?'

'*Si, si, signor Leclercq.*'

'She is absolutely right, of course.' The Director reached for a decanter of red wine and began filling the glasses while his own needs were attended to. 'In preparing a *risotto* there is a brief moment when everything reaches perfection; the moment critique. It is somewhat akin to scrambling an egg or making an omelette; another second and you have left it too late.'

Monsieur Pamplemousse was only too pleased to obey his host's command. The dish was heavenly. The rice must have swelled up to three times its original volume, yet it remained firm and creamy, and the first truffles of the season were beyond reproach. His only regret was that Doucette couldn't share it too.

'Please forgive my digression,' continued Monsieur Leclercq, when they were alone once more. 'Maria is a lovely lady; a trifle taciturn perhaps, but *une perle*, a proverbial "treasure". Like all "treasures" she has her funny little ways and nothing you say or do will change that. Fortunately, her particular talents lie in the realms of gastronomy – so we don't have to put all the pictures straight after she has been round with the feather duster. However she is inclined to appear when you least expect it. For one of such generous dimensions she makes remarkably little noise when she is going about her work. She insists on wearing carpet slippers so that she won't disturb us, but I suspect it is so that she can hear what is going on more clearly.'

'It is far better to be safe than sorry,' agreed Monsieur Pamplemousse.

'"You cannot sew buttons on your neighbour's mouth", as the old Russian proverb would have it,' said the Director.

'Now, to return to the subject in hand...'

Hearing what he thought was the sound of approaching carpet slippers, Monsieur Pamplemousse beat Monsieur Leclercq to it.

'Just recently,' he said, 'I was reading about the late Henry Ford. As I am sure you are aware, his great advertising ploy when the Model T first came on the market was that customers could have any colour they liked provided it was black.'

It was Monsieur Leclercq's turn to look puzzled. 'Yes, yes, Pamplemousse,' he said. 'We all know the reason for that. He wanted to turn out as many cars as he could in the shortest possible time.'

'Ah, but why choose black, *Monsieur*? Why not green or blue, or even red?'

'I really don't know,' said the Director, in a voice that suggested he didn't really care either.

'Because all the other colours took longer to dry,' said Monsieur Pamplemousse.

He felt a wet nose against his free hand. It was Pommes Frites after all. Certain among them were hoping for seconds.

'I will have a word with Maria,' said the Director, noticing traces of rice on Pommes Frites' chin. 'You say he played a role in the whole affair?'

'Without him,' said Monsieur Pamplemousse simply, 'I doubt if we would be sitting here today.

'It was one thing knowing the photographs were in

Madame Chavignol's luggage. Positively identifying the particular suitcase from amongst all the others once it had entered the system would have been another matter entirely. For all we knew there could have been many identical cases being processed. It had to be tagged in some way before she checked in.

'In the event I was able to call on the services of some-one who had actually handled the case and knew which one to look for. I won't bore you with the details, but on the way to the airport I called in at Bon Marché, and for a modest outlay of 1.68 Euros in their food department I purchased a particular brand of almond essence that Pommes Frites identified with the scent inside the oyster shell. He had it fixed in his mind as being a vital clue. He was absolutely right, of course, although the reason wasn't clear to the rest of us at the time.

'By means of subterfuge a liberal dose was planted on the outside of the case before it was checked in, so that Pommes Frites could pick it out with his eyes shut if necessary.'

Monsieur Leclercq produced a tiny dictating machine from an inner pocket. 'I must make a note of that, otherwise we may have trouble with Madame Grante in accounts when you submit your next P.39. Please continue.'

'Through the offices of my ex-colleague in the *Sûreté*, the three of us were able to station ourselves near the plane before the baggage arrived...'

'I have an early edition of *Michelin*,' broke in the Director, 'which has a symbol for hotels that were plagued with bed bugs.'

Taking the hint this time, Monsieur Pamplemousse entered into the spirit of things. 'Squashed or otherwise?' he asked. 'I trust they didn't award the hotels rosettes if it was the latter.'

'No, Pamplemousse, they did not!' said the Director crossly. 'It was meant as a warning.'

Monsieur Pamplemousse heard another shuffling sound behind him. This time it was for real and it was accompanied by yet another delicious smell. Clearly the moment for serious discussion had passed.

Monsieur Leclercq leaned across the table. 'Another window lost,' he hissed.

A bit rich, thought Monsieur Pamplemousse, considering the number of times the Director had monopolised the conversation. On the other hand... the smell drew closer.

'I thought we would meet here so that we would enjoy peace and quiet,' continued Monsieur Leclercq, above the sound of comings and goings from the kitchen. 'My wife is in Paris today visiting a fashion show in the Avenue Montaigne. Chanel, I believe. Let us hope she doesn't bump into Madame Pamplemousse. They may put their heads together and exchange notes.'

'I think that is highly unlikely,' said Monsieur Pamplemousse. He didn't suggest it was more likely to happen in Galeries Lafayette. The irony would be lost.

'*Suprême de pintade et raviolis aux poireaux*,' announced the Director as plates arrived on the table. 'Yet another of Maria's specialities. She uses only the white of leeks, lightly braised to form a base for marinated breasts of guinea-fowl, grilled, as you will see, until they are golden brown, then thinly sliced. The sheets of ravioli covering the whole are homemade. *Crème fraîche*, chicken stock and butter is used to make the sauce. Both the *crème fraîche* and the butter are from Echiré.'

He rose to replenish the glasses. 'I trust you find this wine to your satisfaction...'

'*Parfait, Monsieur.*' Monsieur Pamplemousse had

already identified it as being from the Rhône Valley, but it was not one he'd had the good fortune to come across before.

'It is a Côte Rotie d'Ampuis from Guigal,' said the Director. 'A blend of his six top cuvées. Need I say more? It could hardly enjoy a better pedigree.'

Not for the first time it struck Monsieur Pamplemousse that the Director had missed his vocation. He would have made an impeccable *maitre d'*; especially if Maria had been doing the cooking.

'You are lucky with your "treasure", *Monsieur*,' he said, as she disappeared in the direction of the kitchen.

'Alas, it is only a temporary arrangement,' said the Director. 'Her husband passed away recently and she has no one to cook for. She is simply filling in.'

'He must have died a happy man,' mused Monsieur Pamplemousse, dabbing at his lips with a napkin having sampled the guinea fowl. The Director was right about the sauce. The characteristic nutty flavour of the Echiré *crème fraîche* came through. There was no denying the importance of prime ingredients.

'Those in the village do say he passed away with a smile on his lips and a lump of spaghetti Bolognaise stuck to his chin,' said Monsieur Leclercq. 'Unfortunately she has decided to return to Italy to be with her children. We shall certainly miss her. So what happened next?'

Monsieur Pamplemousse speared another portion of his guinea fowl before continuing. It was a pity to mar the pleasure with too much talk.

'Once the luggage arrived on the tarmac,' he continued after a moment or two, 'Pommes Frites set to work and immediately homed in on the target. From that moment on events followed an established pattern. Any unidentifiable item of baggage is an object of suspicion and treated accordingly.'

'How about labels?' broke in the Director. 'Surely Vuitton supplied Madame Chavignol with a matching set of labels for her name and address.'

'Labels?' said Monsieur Pamplemousse innocently. Reaching into a jacket pocket, he produced a leather-bound tag and handed it across the table.

'As I was saying, a tried and tested procedure is put into place. The object is first removed to a safe location, and the area cordoned off. Explosive material is placed beneath it, and the whole is then covered with sound deadening material.

'It is much like making a *pommes tourte*, except instead of the apple pie being consumed, the explosive device is detonated and the case and its contents blown to smithereens.

'The area is then cleared and tidied up, the tape removed, and life goes on. It has become such a common occurrence it doesn't even get a mention in the press. I doubt if even many people on the plane knew it had happened.'

Monsieur Leclercq reached for a small hand-bell. 'I shall be interested to hear what gave you the idea as to the whereabouts of the photographs in the first place, Aristide. But first we have a little green salad to clear the palate, along with some Pont l'Evêque cheese to go with the rest of the wine.'

Sensing a longer period between their arrival and the serving of the dessert, Monsieur Pamplemousse seized the opportunity to fill in the details, including Claudette's arrival at the airport.

'And you think this Pascal will be joining Madame Chavignol in Marseille?' asked the Director.

'I think she will be joined there,' said Monsieur Pamplemousse non-committally. 'He will be driving down

200

to Marseille in his Facel Vega.'

'In which case, why not take the luggage?'

'The simple answer to that is that neither probably trusted the other.'

'It will not be a happy moment when they eventually meet up,' mused the Director.

'You can say that again,' thought Monsieur Pamplemousse, picturing Claudette waiting by the carousel for her case to emerge. While Monsieur Leclercq was digesting the notion, he helped himself to another wedge of Pont-l'Evêque. It was creamy yellow, glistening with fat and stronger than usual.

'It comes from a small farm in Normandy.' The Director couldn't resist breaking off from his reverie. 'One of the very few, perhaps 2% of the total, who still produce it by hand.'

'Did you know that the man credited with the invention of electronic television in the United States got the idea when he was only fourteen years old?' asked Monsieur Pamplemousse. 'Until that moment people in many other parts of the world had been trying to perfect a means of transmitting pictures with the aid of revolving discs.

'His name was Philo T. Farnsworth and one day he was ploughing a field on his father's farm in Idaho when he happened to glance round to view his handiwork. Seeing the lines of dead straight furrows stretching out across the landscape caused him to wonder about the possibility of breaking up a picture up in the same way, line by line, and transmitting it electronically.'

'I didn't know that, Pamplemousse,' said the Director, pouring the last of the wine. 'But it seems to me to be a particularly useless piece of information in the present context. Why are you telling me?'

'Simply to answer your earlier question, Monsieur, and

to make the point that ideas are often things of the moment, triggered off quite by chance. The muse strikes in surprising ways. Had Doucette not shown me some old snaps taken in Nice it would never have occurred to me where the photographs might be kept.'

'And you really think they have all been blown to Kingdom Come?'

'That is my hope and belief, *Monsieur*, and I see no reason to think otherwise.'

Monsieur Leclereq got up and crossed to the mullioned window. 'It is amazing how a single sunbeam can light up the day,' he said, gazing out at the tranquil scene beyond the boundaries of his estate; orchards shedding their leaves and further still, now that the early morning mist had cleared, there were fields where sheep could be seen grazing. 'There have been moments of late, Aristide, when I feared the worst. I really find it hard to find words to express how much I, and many others, are in your debt.'

'Then I suggest you do not try,' said Monsieur Pamplemousse gently. 'Never forget I also had a vested interest in making sure the photographs were destroyed.'

'And what you are also saying is that now her husband's ashes are safely below ground Madame Chavignol has gone off into the blue with his assistant, Pascal, to begin a new life.'

'I think that is what both of them would like everyone to believe, *Monsieur*.'

'So that is that.' The Director could hardly contain his relief as he returned to the table and began replenishing the glasses.

'Not quite, *Monsieur*. There was another point to my analogy with television. It seemed to me an odd twist of fate that Chavignol chose to use that medium to put his scheme into practice.'

'You have lost me, Aristide,' said the Director. 'Surely, much as one disliked the man one can hardly accuse him of committing suicide on air.'

'No,' said Monsieur Pamplemousse. 'But he may end up facing a charge of murder, or at the very least being an accessory to one. It is my belief that he is still alive. Alive and well and, along with his wife, thinking they have got away with it.

'Furthermore, when the powers that be catch up with events I predict there will be a move to have the ashes recovered.'

'But what would be the point?'

'I think they will find they are Pascal's. They can work wonders in the laboratories these days. Identification will only be a matter of time.'

'I can hardly believe what you are saying,' said Monsieur Leclercq. 'I assume you must have good reason.'

'Several things set my mind working,' said Monsieur Pamplemousse. 'First of all, when I visited Madame Chavignol she told me a direct lie. It probably slipped out and was too late to correct – I did a similar thing when I denied having a card shortly after having shown one to the security camera – but she said she had been watching the programme at home, whereas I know for a fact she was in Chavignol's flat at the studios.

'I think she was there with the express purpose of making sure they weren't disturbed when he was brought up. My belief is that Pascal was already beyond help having died of cyanide poisoning while watching the show with her.

'I think it was more than fortuitous that the normal Staff Nurse was on holiday at the time. I think it was planned that way.

'It always bothered me that Pommes Frites had become

so fixed on the smell of almond essence as opposed to the real thing. The simple truth is that he was right all the time. That was what had been injected into the shell of the oyster used on the show.

'For a magician of Chavignol's calibre the whole thing, the feigning of his death, the carrying out of a quick change into Pascal's clothes before the arrival of the *Sapeurs-Pompiers*, would have been child's play.

'A chance remark by a certain gentleman in a Montmartre sex shop also set my mind working. He mentioned having had a big order from Marseille of all places.

'Then there was the car – the Facel Vega Excellence. It was Chavignol's pride and joy. He would be hard put to find another like it. I suspect that is why early on he planted the fact that Pascal would be getting it when he died.'

'In that case, wouldn't that have been even more reason for them to have gone away together taking everything with them?'

'I think for the time being at least they needed to keep up the pretence that Claudette's relationship with Pascal was still entirely innocent. That was why he was so happy to flaunt himself driving around in it, posing as Chavignol's one time assistant.

'That also aroused my suspicions. By all accounts the Excellence is not an easy car to drive and the night I saw it whoever was at the wheel handled it with great aplomb, which certainly didn't fit in with what I'd been told about Pascal's driving.'

Feeling inside his jacket again, Monsieur Pamplemousse took out some sheets of A4 paper and handed them to the Director.

'More souvenirs, Aristide?'

'Your new camera came in very useful, Monsieur. These are only rough prints on plain paper, but the first picture shows a close-up of some hands on the steering wheel. They are not Pascal's; they are much too delicate. Pascal has the hands of a manual worker. If you look at the second photograph you will see what I mean. It is a printout taken from a television picture of a photo frame in Madame Chavignol's bedroom. At first I thought she was keeping it by her bed because of the association they had formed, but I think the explanation is more prosaic. Chavignol was a perfectionist and he needed it for getting into character; making sure he had a false moustache in exactly the right position. He left nothing to chance.

'The third one was taken at the airport. Once again, you will see it is Chavignol's hands pushing the trolley, not Pascal's.

'Blown-up on the correct paper, I think they will provide crucial evidence.'

'But why? What prompted all this in the first place?'

'I suspect Chavignol knew things were closing in. The *Brigade Mondaine* had their sights fixed on him and they weren't going to give up in a hurry. His time was running out and he couldn't face the thought of being sent to prison, possibly to spend the rest of his life behind bars.'

'Will the two of them ever be found?' asked the Director.

'I think it is only a matter of time,' said Monsieur. 'In some respects the forces of retribution are already at work. They still have each other and that may turn out to be punishment enough. It is another strange twist of fate that to all intents and purposes Chavignol has effectively killed himself off. His wife will inherit all his money, and he doesn't even have the benefit of the photographs to fall back on.'

He broke off as the familiar sound of something being whipped drew near and Maria appeared from the direction of the kitchen clutching a large unlined copper bowl and a whisk.

As soon as she reached the table she began spooning the creamy yellow contents of the bowl into some open-topped glasses.

'*Zabaglione*,' said Monsieur Leclercq, 'made in the traditional manner with egg yolks, sugar and Marsala beaten together over a low heat. As with the *risotto*, it needs to be eaten at once. Is that not so, Maria?'

'*Si, si, Signor Leclercq.*' Maria made a hasty exit only to reappear moments later with a plate of puffed-up fritters, golden brown and fresh from the pan.

The Director gave a sigh of pleasure mixed with sadness. 'It is one of the blessings of France, Aristide, that we are bordered by so many other countries, each with its own distinctive cuisine. Italy, Spain, Germany, Belgium, and Switzerland. In one way and another all of them, even Switzerland with its *fondue*, have influenced our cuisine, but undoubtedly Maria's homeland has contributed most of all.

'In more ways than one, in the short time she has been with us she has given us much food for thought. You could say she has broadened our horizons. It is a shame our Founder never got as far as Italy on his *bicyclette*.'

'She has a wonderfully deft touch with a whisk,' said Monsieur Pamplemousse, scraping his glass clean.

'Do not remind me,' said the Director gloomily. 'Again, she insists on using her own traditional unlined copper bowl. Finding a replacement for her will not be easy.'

He rose from the table. 'I was going to suggest rounding things off with a *digestif*, but in the circumstances I think a celebratory glass of champagne is called for.'

Monsieur Leclercq was gone rather a long time and when he returned he was carrying a glistening bottle in one hand and Maria's copper bowl in the other.

'I thought Pommes Frites might like to join us,' he announced.

'I don't suppose he's ever eaten *zabaglione* before,' said Monsieur Pamplemousse. 'There is a first time for everything.'

He recognised the Gosset label on the champagne. It was his favourite. For all his quirky ways the Director was a kind and thoughtful host. He threw a balloon in the air.

'I was thinking while you were out of the room, *Monsieur*. You have not been over-fortunate with your lady cooks in recent years. There was the English girl, Elsie, the one who specialised in a dish called Spotted Dick. As I recall, she left in somewhat of a hurry. Now Marie. Perhaps it is time to try a change of sex.

'I may be able to put you in touch with someone who will almost certainly be looking for a job. I have sampled his cooking and I am certain it would meet with your approval, although I doubt if his last employers will be able to provide references.'

It was a small return for such a delicious meal; really more of a *quid pro quo*. He didn't mention Monsieur Leclercq had also experienced Yang's cooking, for fear it might prejudice him.

He just hoped the Director's newfound horizons were sufficiently catholic to extend beyond the Western world. If they didn't already, he had a feeling they soon would.

It was his good deed for the day.

The drive back to Paris wasn't the best he'd ever had. There were too many things on his mind. Good things and bad things. One way and another he had hardly stopped all the week. Unlike his 2CV, which didn't exactly bristle with optional extras, his brain was still in overdrive. He wondered if he had been over-optimistic in his report to the Director. He didn't think so. He wondered, too, about Mademoiselle Katz and all the others he had met at the studios; what the future held for them. He also wondered if he would ever be able to eat again. But then, that was often the case after a good meal. In his profession it was something of an occupational hazard.

Pommes Frites also appeared to have a lot on his mind. He was clearly worried about something, and when he was in that mood it was much the same as having a nervous passenger on the back of a motorcycle. He was apt to lean the wrong way and steering suffered accordingly. Several times Monsieur Pamplemousse had difficulty getting round corners at anything approaching his normal speed.

The meal had been beyond reproach; both the food and the wine were memorable. But as for the venue providing an opportunity for peaceful discussion... Fumes apart, Monsieur Pamplemousse couldn't help thinking a pavement café in the Rue de Rivoli would have been a better choice.

One way and another he was looking forward to putting his feet up.

What he didn't expect to find when he got home was Doucette standing in the middle of the hall clutching a spear.

The assegai had been a present many years before from a grateful African witch doctor who had been arrested for playing a tom-tom in a block of flats at two o'clock one morning. Through Monsieur Pamplemousse's good offices the charge of disturbing the peace had been dropped, and the subsequent gift had been standing in their hall for so long he had almost forgotten it was there.

'You won't believe me when I tell you what's been happening,' said Doucette, an unholy gleam in her eye.

'Try me,' said Monsieur Pamplemousse wearily.

'They've been back!' said Doucette.

'They?' repeated Monsieur Pamplemousse, suddenly all ears. 'What do you mean *they*?'

'Those two men who came earlier in the week. Well, not the same two. But they both had clipboards. They spun me some yarn to do with there having been complaints about your *jardinières*. Apparently there is a story going around that one of them fell off the balcony. But that simply isn't possible.'

'You haven't been out there since the first two men came?'

'Should I have?'

'Never mind. What happened?'

'These two are much worse than the others. The first two were perfect gentlemen, but these...' Doucette gave a shudder. 'They practically forced their way in when I tried to shut the door on them. I won't tell you what they said when I drove them into the kitchen.'

'You did what? Are they still there?'

'They have nowhere else to go,' said Doucette simply. 'They are locked in.'

'Give me the key, Couscous,' said Monsieur Pamplemousse grimly.

'I can't.'

'What do you mean – you can't?'

'They have it. They locked themselves in. I think they were a little afraid of what I might do.'

'Have you called the police?'

'I was waiting for you, Aristide,' said Doucette. 'I know how you feel about these things. Aren't you proud of me?'

'How long have they been in there?'

'About three hours. In the beginning they were knocking so loud I thought the neighbours might complain. But they've given up now.'

Monsieur Pamplemousse struggled to find the right words. 'Leave it to me,' he said at last.

Signalling Pommes Frites to stand by, he crossed to the far end of the living room and braced himself to charge.

'Enfants de garce!' he cried, as his shoulder landed fair and square in the middle of the door. 'That is for my *marjolaine!'*

'Salauds!' he shouted at the second attempt. 'That is for my *fenouil!'*

'Sélérats!' he bawled as tried for a third time. 'That is for my *oseille!'*

He was beginning to wish he hadn't started. Apart from the pain in his shoulder he was running out of herbs.

Taking a deep breath, he lowered his head in preparation for the final assault. 'And this...' he cried, as he gathered speed. 'This is for my *estragon!'*

He was over halfway across the room there when the door suddenly opened. Too late to stop, he shot straight through into the kitchen, dimly aware as he did so of two figures going past him in the opposite direction.

'Aristide? Are you alright?' Doucette's cry of alarm was punctuated by the sound of barking and the slamming of a door.

Monsieur Pamplemousse didn't answer. He was sitting on the floor studying a piece of paper. It bore an official stamp.

'Why did you let them go, Aristide?' Doucette came into the kitchen and helped him to his feet.

'Because...' began Monsieur Pamplemousse. He wondered if he should tell her the truth.

By now the men must be halfway to the *Mairie*, with Pommes Frites hot on their heels. They would be back.

Nothing was more certain. Probably with reinforcements. It would be as well to make sure that when they did return there was nothing on the balcony they could complain about.

'Perhaps, Couscous,' he said, 'seeing tomorrow is the last day of my holiday, we could go for a drive in the country. If we leave early we can take advantage of the fine weather. It may be the last chance we shall have before winter.'

It was hardly fate that caused him to follow the same route out of Paris as he had taken the previous Sunday; more a matter of satisfying his enquiring mind.

The census people were still there. Not only that but they recognised him immediately.

'Don't tell me you are going to see your sister-in-law again,' said the man with the clipboard.

'You must be a glutton for punishment, *Monsieur*,' chuckled the *gendarme*.

'There are *three* of us today,' said Monsieur Pamplemousse pointedly. 'Allow me to introduce my wife. You understand what I am saying?'

The *gendarme* was quickest off the mark. 'Of course, *Monsieur. Bonne promenade.*' Coming to attention, he saluted. Clearly he must keep himself abreast of the news. In the old days Monsieur Pamplemousse would have marked him down for promotion.

'Two adults, one *chien*.' The man from the census ticked off his boxes. Then he, too, did his best to salute.

'What was all that about?' asked Doucette, as they drove on their way. 'We are not going to visit Agathe are we? She won't be expecting us and you know how she suffers from palpitations when she gets taken by surprise.'

211

Monsieur Pamplemousse shook his head.

'Thank goodness for that,' said Doucette. 'I really couldn't stand another *tripes à la mode de Caen* quite so soon.'

Monsieur Pamplemousse stared at her. 'Do you mean to say you don't like it either?'

'It is revolting,' said Doucette. 'She only does it to please you. In the beginning she was so delighted we had met. Besides, at the time you said how nice it was.'

Monsieur Pamplemousse narrowly missed running into the back of an articulated lorry. 'Do you mean to say that all these years we've been living a lie and I have been paying for it with indigestion.'

'It's too late to go back on it now,' said Doucette firmly. 'Agathe would be devastated.'

'It was the first time we had met,' protested Monsieur Pamplemousse. 'I could hardly say it was the worst I had ever tasted. I might have lost you.'

Doucette gave his knee a squeeze. 'You know you wouldn't have, Aristide.' She settled back in her seat. 'Anyway, let us not spoil today. It's quite like old times – just the two of us – driving out into the country for no reason at all other than the fact that we like being together.'

'Three.' Monsieur Pamplemousse corrected her. 'Pommes Frites isn't used to being squashed up in the back. He may want to get out and stretch his legs amongst other things later.'

He wondered if it was right moment to mention that what he really had in mind was paying a visit to a garden centre in order to replenish his stock of herbs and buy a new *jardinière*. He decided to wait until he saw the approach signs.

'These things are really all a matter of communication, Couscous,' he said. 'If you want my opinion, lack of communication is responsible for half the ills in this world.'

Glancing up at the rear view mirror he caught Pommes Frites' eye. He was wearing his quizzical expression; half disbelief, half barely concealed admiration. Or to put it another way, he looked like a dog who was finding it extremely difficult to believe his own ears where his master was concerned.